ROMA

ROMA

*Book IV in the Middle
Empire Series*

CONN HALLINAN

Ballingarry Press

To my wife, Anne,
who encouraged me to write this fourth book
in the Middle Empire series.
As always, she was right.
If the Romans had had her,
the Empire would have lasted a lot longer.

Contents

Characters   xi
Prologue   xiii

I   I

II   9

III   12

IV   17

V   22

VI   28

VII   36

VIII

41

IX

48

X

55

XI

64

XII

69

XIII

75

XIV

79

XV

87

XVI

91

XVII

100

XVIII

110

XIX

117

XX

135

XXI

139

XXII

145

XXIII

152

XXIV

162

XXV

168

XXVI

170

XXVII

181

XXVIII

191

XXIX

197

XXX

204

XXXI

213

Glossary of Terms 219
Place Names 220
Roman Currency 221
Structure Of A Roman Legion 222
Bibliography 224
Acknowledgements 227

Characters

Manius Acilius - Roman loan shark

Sabina Aquillius - Marcus's niece

Julia Aquillius - Marcus's sister, mother of Sabina

Lucius Aquillius - Husband of Julia

Cassius Caesernnius - Aelia's lawyer in Roma

Antonius Clodius - Praetorian Guard Tribune

Coventina - Celtic woman, companion of Demaratus

Julius Dasumi - Wealthy Hispania merchant, brother of Aelia

Aelia Dasumi - Julius's sister and companion to Marcus

Gnaeus Domitius - Hired assassin

Vilaus and Numerius - Body guards and Flavius's cousins

Gaius Messius Quintus Trajanus Decius - Emperor

Demaratus, Signifer - Marcus' third in command, a Greek

Publius Felix - Tribune, VII Legion Hispania

Marcus Favonius - Acting Legate, VII Legion Hispania

Tiberius Favonius - Marcus' brother

Aeolus Hadrianus Marullinus - Legate, Praetorian Guard

Gaius Julius Cornutus - Senator helping Aelia

Aulus Nonius - Aide, Praetorian Guard

Quintus Junius - Tribune, VII Legion Hispania

Titus Livius - Aelia's lawyer in Hispania

Quintus Prompeius - Senator, Marcus's former commander
    in Britannia

Flavius Priscus - Optio, Marcus's second-in-command

Faustina Priscus - Flavius's mother
Lucius Priscus - Flavius's father
Rachel Levi - Former slave, adopted sister of Aelia
Timotheus - Doctor, VII Legion Hispania

Prologue

It is 300 years since Julius Caesar conquered Gaul and made it one of Rome's wealthiest provinces, but once again the Empire's legions are fighting desperate battles in the dense forests of the north. Victories no longer signal the end of a war, instead presaging future wars. The myriad tribes Rome once so easily defeated or manipulated have banded together into great confederations that contend almost as equals on the field of battle. While the Empire strains to hold back the floodtide of Goths and Franks pouring across the Rhine and the Danube, fierce Parthian horsemen press in on Rome's eastern borders. Assailed from without by invasion, the Empire is shaken from within by inflation and political upheaval.

The year 252 AD is at the center of the "Middle Empire," that period between the conquests of Julius Caesar and the last stages of the Empire before the Vandals sack Rome in 455 AD. In the Middle Empire, Rome is still immensely powerful, but a careful listener might hear the first whispers of decline and fall.

From the reign of Caracala (211-217 AD) to the Emperor Diocletian (284-305 AD), Rome will have 12 emperors. All but two die by violence, five by murder. Civil war becomes the norm.

As instability grows and trade declines, the Empire shifts from conquest to defending its borders, and the once all-powerful Roman economy begins to falter. For hundreds of years, Rome's economy had depended on the millions of slaves captured through war. But by the Middle Empire those days are a distant memory: Rome's last successful war of conquest was the Emperor Trajan's second Dacian War in 106 AD. The era of cheap slaves is over, and, as slaves grow increasingly expensive, the system's inefficiency and instability accelerate.

As political crisis grips the center, centrifugal forces spin off provinces in the east and north, creating independent Empires in Britannia and Gaul, and Palmyra east of the Levantine coast. But Hispania—Rome's oldest and arguably richest province—remains loyal. It was here that Rome first confronted an enemy as powerful as itself: Carthage. It was here that the Empire began. It was here that Caesar defeated Pompey in the civil war that ends the Republic. And it was here that the western Empire makes its last stand.

In 252 AD, Hispania was a land of vast mineral wealth, and for a time, the Empire's major source of fish, olive oil, and grain. It was an early flashpoint between Christianity and the Roman state. And it produced two of Rome's greatest emperors, Trajan and Hadrian.

Book I, *Hispania*, follows three principal characters. Centurion Marcus Favonius, the youngest son of a politically ambitious family, is fleeing the enmity of the Praetorian Guard. He is accompanied by his second-in-command, Flavius Priscus, a street fighter from the tough slums of Rome. And by Demaratus, the centurion's third in command, a Greek, former sailor, and a man with a keen sense of history and an outsider's view of the Empire he serves. The three evade assassination and establish themselves in Spain's VII Legion.

In Book II, *Mauretania*, the three lead an expedition to what is now modern Morocco to rescue Romans seized by Mauri slave traders. The expedition is a success, and Marcus finds love, but falls afoul of a powerful merchant in Hispania. The book develops two new characters, Aelia Dasumi, a wealthy woman first encountered in "Hispania," and Rachel Levi, a slave.

Book III, *Tarraco*, is based on a Frankish invasion of Hispania, and develops the character Coventina, a Celtic woman introduced in *Hispania*.

Book IV, *Roma*, follows Marcus, Favius and Demaratus, accompanied by Aelia, Rachel and Coventina, to the Empire's capital to pit their wiles against intrigue and assassins.

The VII Legion Hispania Gemina Pia is one of the most interesting units in the Roman Army, and the centerpiece for these books. The VII was an unusual legion, made up of native Hispanians and, with a few exceptions, served on its home territory. The Romans normally assigned legions to areas where they had no local ties or roots, as Rome wanted its legions' first loyalty to be to Rome. The VII, the oldest serving legion in the Roman Army, had an unerring knack for picking the winning side in a civil war.

The VII Hispania Gemina Pia disappeared from the written record sometime in the Fourth Century. It was never officially disbanded, but when the Visigoths overran Hispania (469-478 AD) there is no mention of the VII Legion.

I

Marcus Favonius Facilis, former centurion, former praefectus castrorum, and current acting legate of the VII Legion Hispania Gemina Pia, was being careful. Sitting on a couch in the atrium of the house of his consort, Aelia Dasumi, he was doing his best not to draw attention to himself. The reason for his efforts occasionally passed in and out of the room, with its tiled fountain and naturalistic murals.

He watched Aelia with a certain wariness. She was a woman of boldness, confidence, intelligence and charm, but when she was angry, she was scary. She did not rage or throw things. On the contrary, she grew very quiet. Marcus had been in enough battles to know that the ones you most needed to fear were not those who bit their shields and pounded the ground with their swords, but the quiet ones who watched for an opening to strike.

Aelia's brother, Julius, was the target of her ire, not Marcus, but Marcus had been around war long enough to know that anger had a habit of spilling over into the lives of everyone around it. And Aelia looked ready to strike.

Marcus sighed and reviewed the matter in his mind. It was

complex, to put it mildly.

When Aelia's father died, he had divided his enormous wealth in Hispania between his two children, Aelia and his son Julius, in a will that was unprecedented. Property was always inherited by the eldest male through the rule of primogeniture. Women had virtually no rights. But Aelia's father had a difficult relationship with his son and a warm one with his daughter. So, he appealed to the Emperor Gordian III and the Roman Senate for an exception, and at considerable cost to his treasury, it was granted. Julius was now appealing that ruling, undoubtedly using his wealth to buy the votes of several senators.

Nothing was very stable these days. At the instigation of Phillip the Arab, Gordian had been assassinated by his own soldiers. Phillip, in turn, had been killed by Decius in a battle near Verona.

And there was another complication. When Aelia was kidnapped by slave traders based in Mauretania, Julius had made little effort to ransom her back. In fact, it very much looked like he did his best to see that she remained a slave. She was only returned to Hispania because Marcus and a cohort of the VII Legion successfully extracted her from the slave traders' camp and brought her home. She promptly threw her brother out of their house—with the aid of Marcus, his second-in-command Flavius Priscus, and third-in-command, Signifer Demaratus—and banished Julius from Corduba.

A good deal had happened since that confrontation. Marcus had been elevated to acting legate of the VII Legion following his successful liberation of the city of Tarraco from an invasion by the Franks. Indeed, Marcus was the toast of the province, which actually made his personal life more complex, a situation he tried to explain to Aelia.

While currently commanding the VII Legion, his position as legate was not yet official. The regular commander, Titus Valens, had been felled by malady, severely disabled but not dead. Roma might wait to see if Titus recovered, or appoint Marcus as legate, or give that plum to someone else. It was therefore essential that he remain on the job and move the VII Legion from Tarraco back to Legio, its home base in Hispania's northwest.

But Aelia was set on going to Roma and challenging her brother. She had always relied on her charm and good looks to give her an advantage in business, and she fully intended to deploy that same strategy in politics. Marcus, however, could not let her make that trip by herself. First, her brother was a dangerous man who had already demonstrated his willingness to inflict harm on his sister. Second, Roma was still in turmoil, what with the death of Emperor Phillip and the ascent of the new emperor, Decius.

To let Aelia go unescorted into that chaos was unthinkable. When he raised the Roma trip to her, she'd protested, "You have your responsibilities, Marcus, I have mine. Go to Legio. I will keep you informed." She said this while making up lists of what to take on her travels. "Isn't your family friendly with Decius?" she inquired, adding, "In any case, I will have Rachel," referring to the onetime slave, now her adopted sister, with whom she had returned from Mauretania.

Rachel, like Aelia, was certainly an estimable woman and quite capable of taking care of herself, but not in the madness that Roma was sure to be. It was true that Marcus's family had chosen the right side in the civil war between Philip and Decius, but Marcus was uncertain how much that meant in terms of influence. And, of course, emperors had a tendency to come and go rather quickly these days.

There was also a matter that he had never mentioned to Aelia—the Praetorian Guard. Marcus, his second-in-command, Flavius Priscus, and his signifer, Demaratus, had fled Roma to avoid being arrested by the Guard. With the change in emperors, it was unlikely that the warrant would still be valid, but with the Praetorians one could never be sure. They were a world unto themselves, and his family had already had a run-in with the Guard that cost the life of his brother, Mamercus.

Telling Aelia that he was going to accompany her in order to protect her might produce the opposite effect. His love did not like to be "managed," and she was perfectly capable of telling him that under no circumstances could he come with her. If Aelia made such a decision, all the siege equipment in the world was unlikely to breach her defenses.

He would have to move carefully, lest he raise her suspicions. First, he had to settle the problem of moving the VII Legion. Second, he had to convince Aelia that he had reason to go to Roma, though that might be the easier of the tasks since he had a large family in the empire's capitol. Having reached this conclusion, he sought her out, finding her in the master cubiculum with its great sprawling bed. The house in Tarraco was not nearly as enormous as her domus in Corduba, but large enough for him to take a wrong turn or two.

"Yes. Yes, be off my love," Aelia told him. "We both have much to do. I will expect you for dinner tonight," she said distractedly, studying a vast array of dresses and gowns laid out on the bed and couches. She kissed him quickly and went back to examining her choice of wardrobe. Marcus slipped out and headed for the VII Legion's camp just outside Tarraco's walls.

* * *

Antonius Clodius, tribune of the Praetorian Guard, stared at the scroll he had requested of his aide, Aulus Nonius. He already knew what was in the document, but he needed to refresh his memory. The scroll was almost two years old, and thin on details. It told of two Praetorian assassins who had been found dead in the town of Seguntum on Hispania's east coast. Both men had been pursuing a centurion, Marcus Favonius, and his two companions.

The emperor at the time—Philip the Arab—had ordered the Guard to arrest the male members of the Favonius family for treason. Those deaths must not go unpunished, the tribune knew. The Praetorian Guard relied on a certain mystique to maintain its power. Anything that diminished that was a threat. The Favonius family had challenged the Guard and emerged unscathed. Well, one of the brothers had been killed by the Praetorians, but even that had turned out badly. Antonius glanced at the scroll and located his name—Mamercus, he who had resisted arrest, killing one of the Guard and wounding another. A mob had then set upon the Praetorians, driving them off before they could seize the body.

After the incident, the commander of the Praetorians had decided to refrain from any further arrests, but the assassins had already been dispatched to Hispania, and there was no way to recall them. Both had ended up dead. While there was no defini-tive evidence that the centurion and his men had killed the two Praetorians, Antonius was fairly confident that they had.

Ordinarily, the Favonius family's challenge would oblige the Praetorians to even the score. But in this instance, it was not that simple. The Favonius family had ties not only to Emperor Decius but also to Quintus Pompeius, former commander of the Vigiles and newly appointed Senator. Marcus had served under Quintus and earned several awards for bravery. And it was Quintus who had arranged for the centurion to flee to Hispania. Under Quin-tus, the Vigiles had joined with the Praetorians to cut a deal and remain neutral in the civil war between Philip and Decius. Would the new senator object to the Guard pursuing Marcus? Especially since the Favonius family had been on the winning side of the civil war between Decius and Philip? The tribune weighed his options carefully.

Antonius knew Decius to be a suspicious man—a sensible state of mind in Roma these days—with allies everywhere, Sena-tor Quintus Pompeius prominent among them. Any overt move against a Favonius could cause the Guard trouble, and Antonius was the tribune in charge of taking care that trouble did not touch the Praetorians.

But there was an interesting wrinkle. A rich and powerful merchant from Hispania had recently appeared in Roma in an effort to overturn a will. It appears the man's father had divided his vast wealth between the merchant and his sister, a rare oc-currence. The man's name was Dasumi, and that was what made it interesting. The Dasumi's sister was the consort of Marcus Favonius, the centurion.

Marcus was virtually untouchable at the moment. Not only had he rescued this Dasumi woman and others from Mauri slave traders in Mauretania, but he had recently defeated a Frankish army outside of Tarraco and reestablished Roma's dominion over the city. He was no longer a centurion, having recently been named acting legate of the VII Legion Hispania Gemina Pia. In short, a potentially dangerous man to tangle with.

The Dasumi woman was sure to challenge her brother's claim of primogeniture. If, as was rumored, she was Marcus Favonius' consort, might he accompany her? Marcus was still protected, but that protection might soon be diminished. Decius was preparing to take his son and heir-apparent to confront the Goths, who had breached the Danuvius River and threatened the Roman province of Dacia. Bad things—or good things, depending on how one looked at it—happen to emperors when they campaign far from home. If something happened to Decius, would a new emperor continue to protect the Favonius family? This bore watching.

Antonius had summoned his aide to the office, but he was so deep in thought that he just stared at the scroll while Aulus fidgeted. The young man would have to learn patience. The two were a study in contrasts. Antonius plagued with a middle age paunch, his hair thin and graying. Aulus slim, with a rich head of dark curls. The aide was attempting a beard, but it was sparce and ragged, sabotaged by his youth. The tribune would have to find a way to suggest he lose it without hurting his feelings. He liked Aulus, the son of a very rich senator, which was one reason he had taken him on. But the aide had other virtues to recommend him. Antonius had come to appreciate the young man's attention to detail and his initiative. The beard, however, would have to go.

"Sir?" the aide finally interrupted.

Antonius stared at the young man without seeing him for a moment, then pulled himself back to the present. "I want everything you can get me on the movements and plans of this Marcus Favonius," he said.

II

The two men soaking in the thermal bath could not have been more different.

Optio Flavius Priscus was short-legged, with a long, well-muscled torso, thick arms and shoulders, a square head with a nose that had been broken so many times it was little more than a smear in the middle of his face. Scars crisscrossed his body like a map of the roads leading to Roma.

Signifer Demaratus was long-legged, slim and handsome, with dark hair and large gray eyes.

Both had been quiet for several minutes before Flavius finally spoke up. "We can't let him go by himself. And it's not just Marcus we need to worry about."

"No, I agree, but that might not be easy," replied Demaratus. "You going makes sense. You are Marcus's optio, his second-in-command and acting adjunct. I am just a signifer." In fact, Demaratus did not really have a specific job. When he was signifer of the Second Century, he had kept the unit's books and distributed the payroll. But when Marcus was elevated to command the legion, Demaratus had become part of his staff. Since there was an army of clerks to take care of the books, the signifer was left with no specific duties. This did not bother Demaratus. It allowed him to spend more time with his beloved Coventina.

"The clerks can do the books and the payroll, and Quintus can keep things running until we get back," argued Flavius. "Who is going to raise a protest about a trip to Roma after we liberated Tarraco? I figure we can say the leadership issue for the legion is so unsettled that we need to do some lobbying in Roma. That happens all the time."

Quintus Junius was one of the VII Legion's tribunes. He was old and ready to retire, but quite capable of taking over for a short time. "You are ever the master of army bureaucracy, comrade," Demaratus acknowledged. He ignored the comment about more being at stake than Marcus. Flavius was referring to Aelia's adopted sister, the former slave Rachel Levi. Before the Frankish invasion derailed normal life for the VII Legion, Flavius had asked Demaratus to help him marry the woman. But in the uproar over the fall of Tarraco, any talk of marriage had been shelved.

Something bad could happen in Roma—not at all an unlikely outcome given the current turmoil and the nature of Aelia's brother—and Rachel would be in the middle of it. But it was a delicate subject, and not one Demaratus could tease Flavius about. When it came to Rachel, Demaratus trod lightly.

"But why would I be going to Roma?" asked Demaratus. "Marcus will want to know what that is about"

Flavius took a while to reply. "Marcus needs to know about those two Praetorians," he finally said. "He knows we know something about it, because I warned him off asking about the details. At the time, he seemed to accept that. I think I can argue that the deaths might come up while he is in Roma, and we had better all be there if it does." Marcus knew the Praetorians were hunting for him. His family had supported the usurper, Decius, in the fight against Emperor Philip the Arab. In the long run, the family had made the right choice, and Decius was now emperor.

Demaratus initially bristled at the "we." It was he who had ambushed the two Guards, he who had killed them in Saguntum, not Flavius. But he soon calmed down. Flavius was not one to steal credit for something he didn't do. The optio was simply noting that the two of them had plotted the murders and then kept them a secret. "Marcus is not going to be happy," he said, "and sometimes it is hard to tell how Marcus will react."

"He can be quirky," agreed Flavius. "But we are all in this together and he will understand that." The optio stirred. "We had best be about our business, Signifer. There is much to do."

Both men took a quick dip in the cold pool, put on fresh linens and their uniforms, and left the baths.

III

Marcus tried to concentrate on the documents in front of him, but none were of pressing matters, so his mind drifted. Most were appeals for lost income during the Frankish occupation, but that was a policy question and far above his pay grade. The emperor or the Roman Senate would make that decision, not a local acting legate.

His anxiety over what to do with the legion had subsided somewhat, as he'd received a letter from Tribune Quintus telling him to take time off when he had the opportunity. Legate Titus Valens had not improved, and he seemed unlikely to recover from whatever had afflicted him.

Quintus was ready to step in and see to marching the VII Legion back to Legio, its headquarters in Hispania's western reaches. "The centurions will handle most of the work, Marcus, and the clerks have had nothing to do for weeks," the old tribune wrote. "It will do them good to finally work for a living," he added. "You should concentrate on your own status now."

He heard Flavius in the front room of the tent, called him in, and showed him the letter from the tribune in Legio. "I am thinking of accompanying Aelia to Roma, Flavius, so you and Demaratus will have to hold things together here."

Flavius finished reading the letter and placed it on Marcus's desk. "I am not sure that is wise," he said.

Marcus frowned. "Why is that?"

"Demaratus and I have no authority without you, sir," replied Flavius. "I am still only an optio and Demaratus a signifer. We command no one in Legio outside of our century. We really have nothing to do up there. And we have both decided that you should not go to Roma without us."

"Decided?" said Marcus. "You command no one in Legio, but you decide these things for the Legion's commander?"

"Bad choice of words, sir, but in our opinion, this is not something you should do by yourself," replied Flavius. "We both know how dangerous Aelia's brother is, and I wouldn't put it past him to settle this inheritance business in the simplest way possible. Kill the woman and there is no issue."

Marcus was silent for a moment. "You have a point, optio."

"And there is another matter as well," continued Flavius.

Marcus waited.

"If you recall, there was an incident concerning two members of the Praetorian Guard in Saguntum," said Flavius.

Marcus frowned, "Yes, the two apparently had a falling out and killed one another in a fight," he said.

"No. sir, they did not," demurred Flavius. "Would you walk with me outside the camp, sir?

"What are you saying, Flavius?" asked Marcus, getting up from the desk. "I thought...".

"Sir, this is not the place to talk about this," objected Flavius. "Please, sir."

Marcus gathered his cloak and indicated that Flavius lead the way. The two emerged from the command tent, saluting the sentries and headed for the north gate of the camp. Adding several thousand men to a city trying to recover from the Frankish occupation had seemed like a bad idea, so the legion was quartered outside Tarraco. In a short time the two men were clear of the camp and alone.

"Now, what's this all about, optio?" asked Marcus.

Flavius took a death breath. "Do you remember when I told you we are indebted to Demaratus and didn't tell you why?"

"Yes," said Marcus.

"Those two Praetorians were tracking us, sir. But their warrant was unofficial, so they couldn't ask for any help in apprehending us. Since they couldn't arrest us, they planned to kill us and be done with it. So, we stopped them."

Marcus absorbed this in silence, finally asking "What do you mean, 'stopped them'?"

"I mean we killed them," replied Flavius.

"What?" asked Marcus.

"We faked an injury to Demaratus's horse, and the signifer went into Saguntum and set up an ambush," explained Flavius.

For a long time, Marcus was silent, finally shaking his head. "Tell me how it happened."

"I don't know the details myself, sir. Demaratus did the job and he won't talk about it, which I think is a good idea," replied Flavius.

"And why is that?" asked Marcus, a note of exasperation creeping into his voice.

"The fewer people who know of this, the better," he replied. "That is why we never said anything to you. If you were asked about it, you could answer honestly that you knew nothing about it."

Marcus began pacing, stopped, then paced again. "This complicates everything," he said at last. "If the Praetorians conclude we had anything to do with killing those two, they will try to avenge them."

"Yes, sir, we know that. But the men were going to kill us and not for any wrongdoing of ours, just because an emperor wanted your family eliminated," said Flavius. "We were just defending ourselves. That emperor is now dead. It doesn't seem as if we had a lot of choice, sir."

"That 'choice' is not yours to make. I am in command here," flared Marcus. "We could have confronted the two. There were three of us. I doubt two Praetorians could have overcome those odds."

"No, they probably couldn't, but that would have made things worse," said Flavius, standing his ground. "If we killed them and it became public that would invite the authorities to look at our orders. And, as I told you, those orders were sketchy. The man who wrote them may or may not have had the authority to send us to Hispania. If we killed them and kept it quiet, the Praetorians would eventually have come looking for their two men, and probably blame us in any case if they failed to find them. We think our solution to kill them was the best one, sir."

Marcus stopped pacing and looked at Flavius for a long moment. "This could put Aelia in danger."

"It could," admitted Flavius, "which is why Demaratus and I need to accompany you, sir. You need us."

"I will make that decision, not you, optio," said Marcus. He paced back and forth. "I need to think about this. As for both of you, return to your duties. I will deal with you and the signifer later."

Flavius saluted and went back to the camp, leaving Marcus standing by the road. For a long time, he stood there, deep in thought.

* * *

Flavius returned to his tent and wrote a short note. "Here," he said to a clerk passing by. "Find Signifer Demaratus and give this to him."

The clerk took the note and asked, "Do you know where he is, sir?"

"No," flared Flavius, "find him and earn your pay." The man—really more a boy—cringed and fled the tent. The optio felt a pang of guilt. The clerk was not at fault, but the encounter with Marcus put him in a foul mood. It had worried him. He had not expected to be so summarily dismissed.

IV

Marcus, Flavius and Demaratus faced one another in a small, deserted plaza not far from one of the main gates into the city. The legate crossed his arms and nodded at the signifer. "Tell me what happened," he said.

Demaratus glanced at Flavius.

"Eyes on me, signifer," said Marcus sharply.

Demaratus shrugged. "I had an informant watching the port and keeping tabs on anyone asking questions about the three of us. A boy overheard the two Pretorians asking about three Legionnaires who recently arrived," replied the Greek. "The boy rode all the way from Tarraco to Tortosa to warn us."

"And you and Flavius were going to handle it on your own and not inform me about this?" said Marcus.

"Yes, sir. We knew you couldn't be involved without endangering our transfer to Hispania," answered Demaratus. "We also knew that I was the only logical candidate to kill the two, because involving the optio would raise questions with you about where he was going and why."

Marcus was quiet for a moment. "Was your horse really lame?" he asked.

"No. The lame horse was our device to free me to plan how to attack them."

Marcus was silent for a long time. "What then?" he finally said.

"I pretended I was drunk and introduced myself to the two at a tavern. I told them that you and Flavius had tossed me out, and I was happy to point out where you were staying," said the signifer. "I had prepared a deserted house to look like someone was staying there. When they stepped in, I killed them."

"How did you kill two Praetorians?" pressed Marcus.

"I had concealed a knife. They pushed me into the house in front of them and followed me in. I killed the smaller one first. The larger one was more of a problem, but he died as well in the end," said Demaratus. "I arranged the bodies to look like they had fought, and removed all the props I had used to convince them that someone was staying there. I dumped them in a river outside of town."

"That is why you were injured when you caught up with us, wasn't it?" asked Marcus. "Your horse didn't throw you."

"Correct, sir," admitted Demaratus.

Marcus ran his hands through his hair and paced up and down while the two men remained at attention. Finally, he turned to them. "We were a team," he said, "and you betrayed that team by cutting me out of the decision."

"What we did—what Demaratus did, because he was the one who took all the chances here—we did for the team," countered Flavius. "It was the only way we could preserve the cover we had to be in Hispania. Frankly, sir, we are where we are today because of Demaratus. We owe him our lives and our honor."

"Honor?" said Marcus stopping his pacing. "Honor is based on a lie?"

"Honor is based on the outcome," said Demaratus.

"Did the Greeks invent cynicism along with the philosophy of honor?" snapped Marcus.

Demaratus's face tightened, but he said nothing.

Not so Flavius.

"Our signifer took on two Praetorians, sir, not for himself but for all of us," protested Flavius. "He could have vanished, you know. He's not a lifer like you and me, he is a sailor. Any ship would be happy to have him. But he didn't leave." Flavius paused, "Your anger is misplaced, sir. In any case, I was the superior officer, and I told him to go ahead with it. If there is fault, it is mine."

Demaratus gave Flavius a startled look. He had never seen the optio openly challenge Marcus, and he wasn't quite sure what the reaction would be. There was a long, frozen silence.

Marcus, who had been staring at the ground, looked up. "I am not looking for fault, optio. We have worked together ever since we fought those Franks north of Confluentes. But a team only works when everyone is informed. Both of you cut me out of this."

"What would you have had us do?" asked Flavius.

"Trust me," replied Marcus.

"We do trust you, sir," said Flavius. "But that wouldn't have solved anything and just might have gotten us killed. Again, sir, involving you made it more likely that the whole matter would have gone public, and that was not in any of our interests."

Marcus was silent for a long moment. "Leave me and return to your duties. I need to think about this."

"Sir," said Flavius and Demaratus. They turned and left the plaza, headed for the VII's Legion's camp.

As the two walked, the optio glanced at the signifer, whose face was expressionless. Flavius knew that when Demaratus showed no emotion, it was because he was awash with them. "Don't take that comment about lying personally," he said.

"It was personal, Flavius," he replied tightly.

Flavius chuckled. "Actually, I though the comment was pretty funny."

"It was not your honor being questioned," said Demaratus, then adding "sir" to his reply.

Flavius put his arm out to stop the signifer. "If we said what we did to any other superior officer in this army, we would be under arrest, Demaratus. This was a shock for Marcus, and he is not a great one for surprises. But he is sensible and will come around," said Flavius, "Trust me."

"I have no problem trusting you, optio. I trust Marcus as well. The question is, does he trust me?" said Demaratus. His voice still tight with anger.

"Of course he does," soothed Flavius. "He will come around on this, signifer. Of that I am certain. And he will recognize how much he and I are in your debt."

Demaratus waved his hand. "There is no debt incurred, comrade. Remember, I did this for myself as well."

Flavius put his hand on Demaratus's shoulder. "If you had

only been thinking of yourself, you would have ridden right though Saguntum to the nearest port. You didn't. You put your life on the line for us. Marcus will finally figure that out."

Demaratus took a deep breath. "You know him better than me, Flavius. I defer to your experience." He paused, "So what do we do now?"

"We do what we were ordered to do—get about our duties," Flavius replied.

Demaratus shook his head. "But we really don't have duties anymore. We are Marcus's staff, and right now I don't think he wants us around."

Flavius shrugged. "I am going to get something to eat at that seafood place down by the mole. Want to join me?"

"I would like that a lot," replied Demaratus, and the two changed direction and headed for the harbor.

V

Demaratus was in trouble. Distraction had created a pre-dicament.

He had come back to the modest domus that he and Coventina shared and casually announced that he was leaving for Roma sometime in the next week. His mind was on the confrontation he and Flavius had just had with Marcus, and he was trying to sort it out. And he was also a little bit drunk. First, Flavius had come to his defense over the killing of the Praetorians. He had never seen the optio directly challenge his superior before, and that surprised him. Second, he was both angered and puzzled by Marcus's reaction to the news that he and Flavius had plotted the death of the two Praetorians and not informed him. It seemed so obvious to the signifier— it was the only way to stop the two assassins tracking them. Marcus could not know about it. It had been vital that he not be involved in the plot.

He could understand the acting legate's surprise, but not his invoking the hierarchy of the Roman Army. Marcus was the superior officer and had to approve everything he and Flavius did. Couldn't he see that if he were involved the whole affair would have been harder to cover up, and that would be bad for all of them? This way Marcus could honestly disclaim any knowledge of the two Praetorians' fate. He thought of Flavius and Marcus as friends, and Flavius had acted in that capacity by defending him, but Marcus had acted, not as a friend, but as a superior officer.

"What?" said the tall Celt, breaking into his thoughts.

Coventina was not typical of most of the women in Demaratus's life. She was not beautiful or even very pretty in a conventional way. Built long and rangy, with strong limbs, she was actually an inch or so taller than the Greek. Her hair was short, bristly and red. It had once been long and quite dramatic —it was the only part of herself that Coventina truly liked— but she had cut it off to disguise herself when the Franks had occupied Tarraco.

The Celt had been a member of the now famous Women's Legion of Tarraco that had helped spark an uprising against the invaders, and, in gratitude, the city had set her up in a small house while her uncle's home was being rebuilt. Coventina had burned that house as a funeral byre for her uncle. He had been killed by two Franks who had tortured him in an effort to find out where the gold merchant had hidden his goods. She had killed one of the men and wounded the other, and the Franks had hunted her throughout the city,

Coventina's question brought Demaratus back from his ruminations. He added that he and Flavius were accompanying Marcus to Roma, but that he thought they would only be gone for a few months. He really had not considered how his lover might react to this news. In any case, he was used to women who deferred to men when it came to decisions.

That was a mistake.

His experience with most women is that when they got upset, they cried. Coventina did not cry. What she did was draw herself up to her full height—so that Demaratus found himself looking up at her—and let loose a string of invectives that covered Greeks, males, soldiers and anyone with the temerity to march in and make an announcement that affected her life and expect her to acquiesce.

That last word was not in Coventina's vocabulary.

"You don't understand, my love," said Demaratus. "This is not a subject for discussion. I am a soldier and I go where my superior officer goes. That is what being in the Army is."

"You are not going off to war, Demaratus, you are going to Roma where Marcus has family. This has something to do with Marcus's lover, doesn't it? Everyone knows that her brother has fled to Roma and that he and his sister are at odds. You were there when she threw him out of Corduba, and most people in Tarraco consider him a Frankish collaborator."

Demaratus had saved Coventina from being arrested by the Franks when the Women's Legion had disrupted a market that Aelia's brother Julius had a major role in establishing during the occupation. The market charged usurious prices, and Julius fled the city before the VII Legion arrived to liberate it.

The big Celt did not miss much.

Demaratus refocused. The "orders" tack did not work, or at least not with this sometimes exasperating woman. He would have to tell her why it was essential for him and Flavius to accompany Marcus. Taking a deep breath, he put up a hand and said, "It is very complex, my love."

"And we primitive natives can't sort out 'complex' things?" she flared.

"I didn't say that," said the signifer. "Flavius and I are involved in something we can't talk about. You will have to trust me."

Coventina thought for a moment. "Do you want to spend your life with me?" she asked.

The question took him aback. "That is a very large question," he replied.

"But with a simple answer," she said, "Yes or no."

Demaratus prided himself on quick thinking. "Fast on his feet," was the way Flavius put it. But he was struck dumb by the complexity of replying to Coventina's question. He was silent.

"I am patient, my love, but not forever," she said.

"Yes," he blurted out—surprising himself, "Which is why I cannot talk to you about this matter."

She took his hand and led him to a couch on the atrium. Sitting him down she took both of his hands in hers. "Do you remember when you asked me about the amulet on my necklace?" she asked.

He nodded, though he had forgotten about the incident until this reminder. "You told me that it was a secret and that you would have to know me better before you could talk about it."

"Wonder of wonders!" she said, leaning back, "a man who actually listens to women."

Demaratus said nothing, largely because he had no idea where the conversation was going. Coventina had a habit of disconcerting him, and he had learned that the best way to deal with it was to wait. She would eventually get to the point.

"The amulet is a bear." The Greek knew this because she wore it all the time, even to bed. "And it is my namesake. 'Coventina' is the most powerful creature in the forest. She does not seek conflict, but when aroused she is the most terrible of foes. I called upon her when my uncle died, and she came to me and saw me though my war with the Franks. I tell you this because by naming her to you I weaken myself. To know my personal totem is to give the knower power over me, and I do not do that lightly."

"You honor me," Demaratus said softly. "And I would never use it to weaken you." He had no idea how that would give him that kind of power, but sometimes, he knew, it is best to say the right thing and then be quiet.

She stroked his cheek and was silent for a moment. "Coventina called you to that market," she said. "You may think that is silly superstition, but I know it to be true. I felt her. She guided you. And because of you I could fulfill my oath to strike my enemies and repay them for my uncle's death."

She paused, looking down. "But Coventina is not an easy god, my love. She demands much. She tests her children with loneliness and fear. I was afraid. I knew what they would do to me if I fell into their hands. I even yearned for death," she said. "I still hold that fear, Demaratus. I hope to overcome it someday, but that day is in the future." She paused, then looked him in the eye. "I cannot be without you."

Demaratus felt a wave of affection. He knew the Celt did not like to show weakness. It was not a luxury her life had afforded her. When her mother died, Coventina had taken over raising the family, even though she was little more than a child herself. Her father was disabled from a war wound, and she had to become nurturer and breadwinner at the same time. But Demaratus's affection was tempered by the difficult position Coventina's statement put him in. How would he explain her presence to Marcus and Aelia?

"There are complications, my love," he said at last. "I do not know if you would be welcome."

"I will speak to the lady Aelia and her sister," she replied. "I will explain why I am asking to accompany you. If they do not accept me, I will not go."

Demaratus nodded. His first reaction was to insist that he talk with Aelia and Rachel, but Coventina was right. This was a matter for the women, and if the answer was "no" it would sit better if he were not involved. "All right, I will arrange a meeting."

"No, I will do that," she said with a finality that indicated the discussion was over.

VI

Marcus paced his office, stopped, sat at his desk and stared blankly at several wax pallets and scrolls, then paced again. Why had he reacted to Flavius and Demaratus the way he had? Yes, he was surprised, but he knew something was afoot between the two of them ever since they had left Tortosa bound for Corduba. Flavius had even hinted at it when he explained there were some things it was best for Marcus not to know. The two men had acted as friends when they decided to kill the Praetorians and not tell Marcus about it—well, it was also in their interests— and their logic for doing so was hard to argue with. Marcus, like any Roman officer, was invested in the chain of command, but Marcus had bypassed that chain on many occasions himself. So why was he suddenly acting like a by-the-rules officer chewing out a junior tesserarius?

He knew the answer, of course, and it didn't have much to do with command prerogatives. He was feeling out of control. Aelia was preparing to go to war with her brother, and he was not clear what his role would be in that coming conflict. He loved his family, but he was apprehensive about what they were up to with Roma in such turmoil. Added to that was this business with the Praetorians. Flavius and Demaratus may think they had hidden their tracks, but he doubted that the commanders of the Guard would be fooled. But instead of putting his head together with his two subordinates, he was dressing them down like they had made a mistake on a drill field maneuver. He sighed. It was easier to be a centurion and command a century than to be an acting legate in charge of a legion. He would have to fix this.

Life, he thought, was complicated.

* * *

Flavius sat in a warm bath and reviewed matters. He was initially surprised by Marcus's reaction, but when he thought about it, it was understandable. His commander was under enormous pressure. There was the question of Marcus's appointment. He should be given the legate position, but there were lots of richer and more politically well-placed people in the army who would like nothing more than to be in command of a legion in a wealthy province, particularly one that had just successfully beaten off a Frankish invasion. While Flavius was only vaguely familiar with Marcus's family, he knew they were deeply involved in politics, a profession infinitely more dangerous than fighting wars. And lastly, Marcus's lover was girding her loins for a fight with her rich and powerful brother.

The optio had learned long ago not to take rebukes to heart. Let them slide off you, in time most of them go away. Marcus was a sensible officer—and a friend—and he would eventually come around. Flavius was more concerned with Aelia's adopted sister, Rachel.

He had met her under rather strange conditions. When the VII Legion's First Cohort had attacked the slave raider's camp to free Aelia and other Hispania captives, he had cut his way through a tent wall, only to be knocked to the ground by Rachel, who—until Marcus called her off—was about to run a spear through him. It was almost love at first stab. Flavius had been deeply taken by her ever since.

Flavius had asked Demaratus to be a marital intermediary with the former slave, and the signifer had agreed. But when the Franks took Tarraco and the VII Legion went to war, any talk of marriage was shelved.

But now he was going to Roma—Flavius was certain that Marcus would eventually realize he needed his second- and third-in-command with him—and Rachel would almost certainly accompany Aelia. Hence, he would be in close contact with her with nothing at all settled. He would have to talk with Demaratus about what to do. But wouldn't that be a distraction when much weightier matters were at stake? He ran his hands through his hair.

Life was complicated.

* * *

Rachel contemplated a room filled with clothes, everything from delicate silk shifts to cloaks and boots. Aelia had asked her to help choose, but Rachel felt overwhelmed. Seeing heaps of clothing was hardly new to her. Having been a favored household slave, she knew about wealthy Romans' taste for endless garments and accoutrements. But Aelia was in a class by herself.

And this was just the final selection. Altogether, Aelia had enough garments to clothe a small city.

Maybe not so small.

It was times like these that Rachel felt the weight of her former status. Aelia thought nothing of the enormous wealth needed to purchase such a layout, while Rachel had difficulty amassing more than two or three things to wear. Indeed, it was an ongoing point of tension between the two women. Rachel was uncomfortable with wealth, while Aelia felt criticized by Rachel's reluctance to expand her wardrobe. Rachel smiled to herself. She had everything she wanted and yet... was something missing? She didn't know.

She made herself start to organize Aelia's clothes, deliberately choosing several of each type of garment. Eventually she had an extensive selection, which she carefully piled in one part of the room. Aelia was out, so there was nothing she could do about winnowing down her pickings. She retreated to her cubiculum and began laying out her own clothes on the bed. It made for a very small package. Aelia had given her a selection of jewelry and she picked through it, feeling awkward about what was appropriate and what was not.

Flavius. The man came unbidden into her mind. She put aside her task and went into the small garden of the villa and thought about him. What did she think? She was hardly clear. He was not much to look at, with his blunt features and smashed nose, but he was not unattractive. Ordinarily, Rachel would not have given the man a second thought, but Aelia had pointed out that Marcus's second-in-command was clearly smitten with her. And Flavius was smarter than he looked. In appearance he was a street tough, but in conversation he proved thoughtful and, in a limited way, well informed. He had freed her from slavery, and he was also Aelia's lover's best friend.

But he was not Jewish and that was no small thing. She did not take her beliefs or her community lightly. She sighed.

Life was complicated.

* * *

Aelia was trying to focus on what Titus Livius was saying, but lawyers had a way of droning on in vocabulary specific to their profession and elusive to outsiders. Well, to be fair, that was true of all professions. She took a deep breath, then asked, "In simple terms, what are the chances that my brother can break our father's will?"

"This is not a simple matter," responded Titus. He was a sleek, polished man, dressed in a finely made toga. He sported several rings, including an opal the size of a small grape. An intricately designed bracelet, inlaid with silver and gold, graced his right wrist. Aelia had no great admiration for lawyers, but Titus had been a friend of the family for a long time, and her father considered him honest.

"The emperor and the Senate approved it, isn't that simple?" she asked with a tone of wearied exasperation.

"Emperor Gordius III is dead, and the Senate can change its decision," he answered, "and keep in mind that the original will was highly irregular. Women simply do not inherit equally. When your father made that will he flew in the face of hundreds of years of law."

"So, my chances are good or bad?" she persisted.

"Not good, but not impossible," he replied. "It is not a small thing to overturn an act of the Senate or an emperor, even one that is dead. It sets a bad precedent. The Senate is no longer a powerful body. Its membership has prestige, but emperors do not listen to it very much. And your brother is wealthy and buying influence."

"I am wealthy, and I have influence as well," said Aelia, "and I am not tainted by scandal. My brother tried to keep me in slavery and collaborated with the Frankish invaders. That is why he fled Hispania."

Titus shrugged. "The Frankish seizure of Tarraco was a significant matter for Hispania, not for Roma. It was not a real invasion and no real threat to the empire. It is true your brother is not in good odor here in Tarraco, but how much does Roma care about that? Not a great deal I would think, particularly if his appeal is accompanied by significant bribes. It takes one million sestertii to buy a senate seat and many senators have gone into debt to purchase their seats. Your brother could ease that debt."

"So much for law," Aelia said cynically.

Titus spread his hands. "You have resources, Lady Aelia, you will have to deploy them." He paused, and then added "and there is the role of the Vestal Virgins."

"Yes?" asked Aelia, sitting up a little straighter.

"The Virgins are the keepers of contracts and important agreements," he said. "They have the power to influence decisions relating to wills. At least in theory, they can preserve them or reject them."

"But how much sway do they have? Would they defy the

Senate or the Emperor, and if they did, would anyone pay attention to them?" asked Aelia.

"To go against the Virgins is to challenge an institution that goes back to our founding. Their word is sacrosanct," replied Titus. "But I am a local lawyer. You need a lawyer in Roma who knows the ins and outs of the Senate and is well versed in testaments and wills."

"Does such a man exist?" asked Aelia.

"There is someone who can answer that question, Aelia," replied Titus. "Lucius Salvius is well-versed in the ways of the Senate, and he is honest. I knew him while I lived in Roma and have maintained a correspondence with him. I can send you an introduction to him."

"That would be much appreciated, Titus. It appears I will need whatever help I can get," she said.

"You also have some influence through your..." Titus hesitated, looking for a word, finally venturing, "relationship with the man who defeated the Franks and liberated Tarraco. My sources tell me his family is not without influence with the new emperor, Decius."

"Hmmm," said Aelia, "he did not mention that."

Titus shrugged. "He may not have a good relationship with his family, but his recent triumph will reflect well on any who are close to him."

Aelia rose, tossing a small leather bag that clinked on Titus's desk. "I thank you, Titus, for giving me much to think about and for your introduction to the Roman lawyer."

"My pleasure, Aelia, and may Fortuna smile upon you."

Aelia shrugged on her cloak and took her leave, climbing

into the curtained litter outside Titus's domus. She had much to consider.

Life was complicated.

VII

Tiberius Favonius cast a critical eye on the scroll he had just finished writing. Since it was addressed to the new emperor, it needed to be perfect. "To Emperor Gaius Messius Quintus Trajanus Decius, your loyal servant Tiberius Favonius sends you greetings." It went on for several lines before getting to his request at the very the end—a meeting with Rome's new ruler.

Tiberius had no illusions. The Favonius family was "loyal," but not particularly wealthy. They were members of the old equestrian class and were now looking for a favor. He thought about slipping into the letter the fact that his brother, Mamercus, had died at hands of the Praetorian Guard that had been sent to arrest him for opposing Emperor Philip. Decius had killed Philip in a battle near Verona. He also considered mentioning his brother Marcus's recent triumph over the Franks at Tarraco. He held off on both.

He considered why he had done so. His brother Mamercus had died essentially defending Decius, or at least opposing Philip, but the involvement of the Praetorians made the whole issue a thorny one. The Guard had remained neutral in the clash between Decius and Philip, and no emperor could rule without them. The Praetorians were dangerous. Emperors Balbanus and Piplenus had both fallen to the knives of the Guard. How would Decius weigh "loyal" against his own interests? Tiberius was not sure what the answer to that would be.

As for Marcus's victory in Hispania, that too was wrapped up in some very complex politics. How had Franks gotten so deep into the Empire without being challenged? The only possible answer was that someone had let them. Who? And how powerful were they? They had enough authority and influence to neutralize several legions that stood in the Franks' path. What had they hoped to accomplish? Did they include influential families in Hispania? And did Decius know about the matter beforehand?

There was also the arrival in Roma of the fabulously wealthy Julius Dasumi, who Tiberius's sources told him was challenging a will. And not just any will, but the highly unusual will that split his father's estate between him and his sister, who was also Tiberius's brother's companion. Apparently, Dasumi was already spreading his wealth around the Senate in an effort to get that body to reverse a controversial ruling allowing an equal division between the two siblings. The Senate did not have much power these days, and the emperor could always overrule it, but was that in Decius's interests?

Tiberius wanted to move up in the world, and, as the eldest brother, he was responsible for the family. One did not advance by making enemies. If there was opportunity here, there was also danger. It was best not to remind the emperor about the Franks and his brother.

He made sure the ink was dry, folded and sealed the letter,

and called for a house slave. He gave the young man instructions about delivery and sent him on his way.

Two young boys dashed by his office headed for the garden—Julius and Sergius, his sister Julia's two sons—followed at a more leisurely pace by her daughter, Sabina. He found the girl annoying. Sabina was far more interested in politics than playing with dolls or tending to her weaving. In the last year she had begun to leave girlhood behind. She took after her mother, who, while still attractive, had begun to look rather matronly. His sister was intelligent, but intellectually disengaged and overly concerned with appearance and status. Her husband, Lucius, was simply stupid.

Sabina was slim, tall for her age and sex, and beginning to blossom into a young woman. Gray-eyed, with a handsome nose and prominent cheek bones, she was quite fetching. She was also smart and a careful collector of gossip in the streets and market-places. Indeed, there were times when the young woman was better informed than he was. Where she came by this interest in politics he couldn't imagine.

Julia followed her brood, slipping into his office to give him a peck on the cheek. "Marcus is coming!" she said. "Isn't that exciting? He is a hero of the empire, brother. The Senate should give him a triumph, don't you think?"

"Times are uncertain, Julia, and I suspect the Senate has much on its mind," he answered. Of course, the Senate would never order a triumph over the mere relief of a city. He also suspected that certain senators knew a good deal more about the Frankish invasion than they were admitting. Rumor had it that that there was discussion of a "Gaulish" empire that would include Britannia and Hispania, and the Frankish invasion was somehow tied up in that, though exactly how Tiberius had yet to work out.

"Well, you have influence now dear brother, and you should use it to advance our family's fortunes," she said. "You know, Sabina has been in correspondence with Marcus, and he has told her all sorts of things that I wager would be of interest to our new emperor."

"Really? I will have to talk with her about it," said Tiberius, mentally making a note to corner his niece at the first opportunity.

"I will fetch her straightaway," said Julia, departing. "She gets bored playing with her brothers anyhow."

A few minutes later Sabina poked her head into the office and greeted him. He gave her a hug and asked her sit with him.

"Your mother tells me you have been corresponding with Marcus, Sabina. Tell me how he is. I have not had the opportunity to write to him given the upheaval in Roma these days," Tiberius said with a smile.

Sabina simply stared at him. "He is well," she said at last.

Tiberius frowned. "That is all? Just well?"

"He writes about small things, uncle, just everyday life," she replied.

"Surely he must have written you about his military success," continued Tiberius.

"Not a great deal, uncle. I believe he thinks it is a not a proper subject matter for me."

"I should like to read his letters," said Tiberius "Can you send them to me?"

Again, she hesitated. "I did not keep them, uncle, because they were about unimportant things. If I get another before he comes, I will save it," she assured him. "Can I go play?"

"Yes, of course," he answered. Sabina gave him a brief hug and left.

That, he thought, was an odd conversation. Sabina seemed uncomfortable talking with him about Marcus's letters, and Tiberius did not believe her about throwing them out. Why? She appeared to be thinking about how to respond to his questions and then giving him minimal information. What was that all about? What was in those letters? He did not like being stone-walled by a little girl. Well, maybe not so little. She must be close to thirteen, time to be looking for a marriage partnership that would be of political and economic value.

He would ask Julia to find Marcus's letters and bring them to him. In the meantime, he had a number of things to attend to.

Life was complex.

VIII

The door knocker—an ornate Medusa's head—sounded twice, then twice more. Because she was passing by, Rachel moved to answer it. Normally, a household slave would perform that task, but Rachel could not rid herself of the habit of doing things for herself, nor did she want to. It was a source of tension with Aelia, who explained that it was the job of house slaves to answer the door—and prepare food, set and clear tables, pour wine, dress their masters and mistresses, and so on and so on. Rachel, though, felt more comfortable doing things for herself. This, in turn, made Aelia feel judged, which occasionally led to quarrels. But not often. The two women liked one another, and they had been through much together during their captivity in Mauretania. But both were stubborn and neither liked to back down. Well, Rachel was going to answer the door in any case, although a house slave was already coming through the atrium to that end.

She opened the door to a tall woman with short red hair wearing a long dress and cloak, pinned near her throat with a clasp of complex runes. The woman looked her over, clearly considering how to proceed. "Would you tell the mistress of the house, Lady Aelia, that I wish to speak with her," she said.

Rachel was annoyed. The woman had clearly taken her for a slave. That should not have bothered her. Rachel was not ashamed to have been a slave, but the assumption and the tone of the woman's voice angered her. "Aelia is very busy. Leave your name and she will contact you when she has the time," she said coldly.

The woman flushed.

"Good, I have angered her," thought Rachel.

The woman took a deep breath and bunched her fists. "It is essential that I speak with Lady Aelia and her sister. I am Coventina, the companion of Demaratus, and the matter I need to discuss with them is pressing," she said.

Rachel was startled. This was the lover of Demaratus, the woman who had helped free the city of Tarraco from the Franks? "I am Rachel," she hurriedly confessed.

The woman laughed and shook her head. "Then forgive me. I assume that anyone who answers the door to a house such as this is a slave. The Romans have so many of them and they seem to do everything." She paused and took a long look at Rachel. "You are the woman who fought the Mauri slavers. I honor you."

That little speech threw Rachel, who managed a flustered "yes," then awkwardly managed to add, "as Tarraco honors you." She was having difficulty seeing Coventina and Demaratus together. The Greek was handsome and smooth, this woman tall and rangy, and not very attractive, although her appearance was certainly arresting. And her comment on slaves was an uncanny parallel to what Rachel had been thinking when she went to answer the door.

"I know I have come without notice, Rachel, but I need to speak with you and Aelia because time is very short. My Demaratus is preparing to leave for Roma, and I need to discuss something with you both," Coventina explained. "Do you know when you and Aelia might be available?"

"Please come in now, and forgive my initial response. I had no idea who you were," said Rachel, standing aside.

Coventina laughed again. "If a tall woman with no hair showed up at most doorsteps in this neighborhood, they would call a bodyguard, although from what my Greek has told me, you don't need one," she said, adding, "Flavius tells me you pinned him to the ground with a spear. We could have used you in Tarraco."

Rachel colored. She was beginning to like this big, plain-spoken woman. "Come. Aelia is here. We will have to break into her packing." Rachel led them through the atrium and a spacious back corridor to Aelia's cubiculum. She was standing amidst an enormous pile of clothes, selecting some, discarding others. She looked up with a frown, clearly annoyed at the interruption.

"Aelia, forgive us for disturbing you. This is Coventina, and she needs to speak with us," said Rachel.

Aelia's face went through much of the same range of expressions that Rachel's had—initial annoyance, wariness, followed by a certain look of disbelief. *This odd-looking woman is Demaratus's great love?*

Coventina was looking around with disbelief as well,

muttering "By the gods." This comment did not endear her to Aelia, who uttered "Yes?" in a tone that made Rachel flinch.

The Celt looked Aelia over and shook her head. "Looking at you I would never have taken you for someone who could bring down a Mauri warrior all by herself. If you were of my tribe, we would have awarded you a golden torc and a whole roasted ox."

Aelia's expression immediately changed, and her tone shifted from frosty to friendly. "Thank you," she said. "How can we help you?"

Rachel suppressed a smile. Coventina's directness had charm.

The Celt drew a deep breath. "I do not know what Demaratus has told you about my time in Tarraco before he arrived."

"Some things," said Aelia. "He said you killed an invader who had tortured your uncle and, later, a soldier who challenged you. He also said you caused a riot that helped to weaken the Franks' grip on the city." She turned to Rachel, "Sister, do you know more?"

"Only that you were with Demaratus when he seized the ships in the harbor," offered Rachel. "Marcus said that was a major reason why the Franks agreed to talk. He said you were a heroine."

"I was one of many women who planned that riot. I played only a small part in setting it off," said Coventina. She stared at the ceiling as if gathering her thoughts. "Heroine," she said quietly. "That word conceals much. It hides the fear that makes your body stink and your bowels turn to water, that makes it hard to breathe. I felt all that and more when they were hunting me. But we are not supposed to speak of those things lest they tarnish the illusions of others."

Rachel and Aelia were silent. Coventina brought her eyes back to them. "I have not cast aside those fears. They lie in wait for me when I am alone, more so when it is dark. I am afraid to fall asleep because of my dreams. Demaratus is my lamp. When he is there, the horror retreats, and when I awake from my dreams and see him there, I can exhale. One day I hope to overcome this dread, but that is a day sometime in the future."

"What you are saying is that if Demaratus goes to Roma, you must go as well," said Rachel, simply.

Coventina nodded. She looked drained. It must have been difficult to open herself up to strangers, thought Rachel.

"Have you discussed this with Demaratus?" asked Aelia.

The Celt smiled. "'Discussed' might not be the right word, but he is willing to take me depending on what the rest of you decide."

"There is only Rachel and myself to make that decision. Marcus said he intends to accompany us, but we are determined to go whatever he does or does not. You would be part of our party, not his," said Aelia. She looked over at Rachel, who nodded in the affirmative. "And if the signifer comes with us, then so shall you. Welcome."

There was a glimmer of moisture, which she quickly mastered, in Coventina's eyes. "Thank you," she said.

The three women embraced.

"Have you given any thought to what you intend to bring with you? asked Aelia.

"I have not much to bring," said Coventina. "The clothes I wear and a few other things. Most of my clothes were lost in the fire."

"Then you must buy new ones," said Aelia. "Roma is a more formal place than Tarraco or Corduba, particularly for women. Stollas and a pella are required.

Coventina nodded but looked lost. Rachel intervened. "I know a store that stocks such garments, Coventina. I would be happy to show you where they are and to shop with you," she said, adding, "One should never shop alone."

"Why is that? asked Coventina.

"A companion will tell you whether a garment looks good on you or is a disaster," interjected Aelia. "I will tell the shop to send me the bill."

Rachel flinched.

Coventina drew herself erect. "That is most generous of you, Aelia, but I can pay for my own clothes," she said evenly.

"Of course," said Rachel, in an effort to smooth over the friction that Aelia's offer had sparked. Rachel knew that Aelia meant the offer as an act of generosity, oblivious to the potential insult it contained. The casual presumptions of wealth was one of Aelia's more annoying traits, and one that Rachel had to deal with on a regular basis. "We only made that offer because it is we who are insisting on your buying new clothes, so we felt a certain responsibility for the demand."

Aelia looked sharply at Rachel, then, mastering her emotion, said, "Of course. I will leave you to your shopping and get back to my work. It was a pleasure meeting you, Coventina."

"And I am happy to meet you as well, Aelia. I was also serious about the torc and ox, although you might want to refuse the animal," said Coventina, surveilling the house.

On hearing the torc and ox comment, Aelia visibly relaxed.

"This odd-looking woman is good," thought Rachel, admiring the deft way that Coventina had diverted Aelia's response to the Celt's implied rebuke.

"I strongly agree," said Aelia. "The house barely fits the two of us, let alone an ox." She turned back to the garments arrayed on her bed. "I will leave the two of you to your shopping."

As they were leaving, Coventina turned to Rachel. "Do you always get in between her and others?" she asked.

Rachel froze. The woman had spotted what she had done and then come straight out and called it. The combination of insight and bluntness was unnerving. She was both angered and impressed, and she began to get an inkling as to why Demaratus might have fallen in love with this woman. Simple she was not, and Greeks were drawn to the complicated. "She is a good person," said Rachel evenly.

"I am sure she is," said Coventina, "and I know she meant no insult, but if I do not pay my way, then I am not in charge of myself. Apologies for my presumption and lack of tact."

Rachel grinned. "Enough apologies," she said. "At this rate we will never get anything done."

"Let us be off," said Coventina. "I need to stop by my domus and get more money. And then you can tell me how awful I look in whatever I try on."

IX

"Sir, they are here," said the clerk.

Marcus glanced up from a tablet listing the expenses run up by the VII legion's cavalry arm. His clerk, Lucius Tarius, stood at attention. Marcus liked Lucius, who was efficient and capable, if a trifle young for the position of Legion head clerk. It was a post where one could make some money—Marcus had, on occasion, slipped clerks a denarius for jumping him to the front of the line—but he suspected that Lucius did not do that. "Earnest" best described him. He would like to take the young man with him to Roma, but the clerk's knowledge of the Legion's workings was needed at headquarters.

"Show them in, Lucius," said Marcus, "And then go fetch me some olive oil and bread and call in Doctor Timotheus, please." The man saluted and exited to the outer tent. Marcus wasn't hungry, and it wasn't really necessary for the doctor to come to him, but he wanted no one in the command tent for the next half hour.

A few moments later, Flavius and Demaratus marched in and saluted. The Greek was stone-faced, watchful, Flavius, respectful and relaxed. Marcus suppressed a smile. Demaratus was still smarting over his dressing down and not sure what Marcus was going to say. Flavius, knowing Marcus well enough to sense that his summons was a peace effort, had let the rebuke slide off him. Was he that transparent? Marcus wondered.

"We are all bound up in this matter, comrades," he said quietly.

"Yes, sir," both answered. Demaratus visibly relaxed. Flavius remained unperturbed.

"First, is there anything else you haven't told me?" asked Marcus. "I want no more surprises."

Both men glanced at each other, then shook their heads. "No, I think you know what we know," answered Flavius.

"There is nothing that ties you to the deaths, signifer?" asked Marcus

"Only circumstance, sir. We were on the road to Corduba at the same time. But I was careful. I am not saying they cannot make an accusation, but proof will be hard to come by," he replied.

"Good. I suspect the Guard will assume we had something to do with it, but without proof they cannot charge us," Marcus said. "But that doesn't mean they will forget about it. The Praetorians are more than capable of acting on their own."

"Doesn't your family have some influence with the new emperor, sir?" asked Flavius.

"They claim to, but I am not sure we can rely on that. My niece informs me that my brother is maneuvering more for himself than for the family," Marcus answered.

"The little girl?" said Flavius. "What would she know about those things, sir?"

"She is no longer a little girl, Flavius, and she is smart and observant. Her letters are filled with gossip and rumors, but they are the gossip and rumors that the Empire runs on," said Marcus.

"There is one complication, sir," said Demaratus.

"And that is?" replied Marcus.

Demaratus looked uncomfortable. "Coventina has asked to accompany us, and I fear I do not have much choice but to include her. She is still," he hesitated, searching for a word, "delicate, sir. She has nightmares about the Franks. She plans on talking with Aelia and Rachel. If they say 'no' she will not go, but she is a persuasive person."

"It could be dangerous," put in Flavius. "The Praetorians don't much care who they kill."

Demaratus nodded, "I know. I have to say I am uncertain how to proceed."

"That's a first," said Flavius, waving off Demaratus's annoyed reaction. "Okay, signifer, I couldn't resist. But you are right. How we protect Aelia, Rachel, and now Coventina is not obvious. For one thing, we must be armed at all times, but we may also need help."

"Swords are forbidden to everyone except the Praetorian Guard. As regular army, however, I doubt anyone would challenge us. Nevertheless, we should be discreet. Hide your gladis under a cloak and keep a hidden pugio," said Marcus. "And what do you mean, 'help'?"

"I have family in the city," volunteered Flavius. "With the exception of a cousin who is in the Guard, none of them have served in the Army, but they can take care of themselves. We might want to call on some of them to act as bodyguards," he added. "We would have to pay them something."

"Payment won't be a problem," said Marcus, "but our companions might be."

"How so?" asked Flavius.

"We are accompanying these women, but we do not command them," he answered. "Am I wrong in suggesting that 'independent and headstrong' might be the appropriate words to describe all three of them?"

"Yeah," said Flavius. "I seem to remember having a spear right about here," he said, rubbing his throat. "And Aelia killed that Frank all on her own."

"Arguing with Coventina is like disagreeing with a bear," added Demaratus. "You had best do it from a safe place."

Marcus ran his hands through his hair. "So, we are agreed. We will be armed at all times and prepared to defend the three women. And Flavius, you will investigate adding some bodyguards when we need them." The legate paced a bit. "We need to move quickly. Aelia's brother is certainly in Roma by now and using his wealth to tip the scales. We also don't want to be in Roma during the summer."

Demaratus frowned. "Why is that, sir?"

Both Marcus and Flavius laughed. "Because, signifer," said Flavius, "the summer is hot and filled with fevers and diseases. No one stays in Roma from July to September if they can avoid it. Plus, all the good festivals are in April and May."

"It is a magnificent city with lots of sharp edges, signifer," added Marcus. "One pays attention at all times, in particular after dark."

Flavius put a hand on Demaratus's shoulder. "Comrade," he said with a grin, "there are places in Roma where we wouldn't take the VII Legion because we might not get it back."

"And this is the capitol of an empire?" said the Greek, shaking his head.

"Toughens you up, signifer. If you can survive Roma, the Goths, Franks, Mauri and Parthians are a stroll in the woods," said Flavius.

"All right," said Marcus, breaking into the back and forth between his two officers, "let's go to work."

The two saluted and, exiting, passed the entering clerk loaded with oil and bread and trailing the doctor. Timotheus and Demaratus exchanged a quick greeting—Greek solidarity—and the signifer and optio headed for their barracks.

"Sir, where would you like this?" asked Lucius, glancing around for a place to unload the bread and olive oil.

Marcus pointed at his small desk. "There will be fine," he said, "and now I need to talk with the doctor," effectively dismissing the clerk who vanished into the front tent.

"Sir," said Timotheus. The doctor was short—even by Roman standards—slim and good looking.

"Doctor, you are well?" asked Marcus politely.

"Yes, sir. And most of the wounded from the battle at the Frankish camp are healing or already discharged. You read my report?" he asked.

"Yes," Marcus lied. It was almost certainly piled up on a chest near his desk, but he just had not had time to catch up with all the leaf letters, scrolls and wax tablets that plague legion commanders. "You are to be commended, doctor. The Legion and the Empire thanks you."

The man nodded. The last line was proforma for everyone from fighting officers to cooks.

"As you know, doctor, I am not in love with ocean travel," said Marcus.

The man nodded. "I do recall that, sir. Are you contemplating a voyage?"

"I am," said Marcus, "Of several days. I believe you prepared a drink from poppy seeds that made our trip from Mauretania to Hispania considerably more pleasant than our voyage there."

"Yes, sir. I can make you a potion that will dampen the symptoms of sea sickness. I will do so immediately," he said.

"Thank you, doctor," said Marcus, "and one more thing. Do you have an antidote for poison?"

Timotheus arched an eyebrow. "Headed for Roma, sir?"

Marcus laughed. "Yes, and, as you know, that is a place filled with all sorts of poisons, most of them in human form."

"My answer is 'yes,' but if you want one that works, I am afraid there is little I can do," said the doctor.

"Explain," said Marcus.

"The recommended antidote for poison is mithridatum, a combination of over six drugs and herbs. The only problem," said Timotheus, "is that it doesn't work."

"I have heard of it, and I thought it was well accepted as an antidote," said Marcus.

"Lots of remedies are 'accepted,' sir, but that doesn't mean they do anything. Mithridatum is one such drug. If you like, I can prepare a supply of it, but I would not rely on it to save anyone," Timotheus replied.

"What do you suggest?" asked Marcus.

"Be careful what you eat and drink," said the doctor. "A feather down the throat can induce vomiting, which is the best way to counter poison."

"Prepare me some mithridatum, doctor, and I will bring a supply of feathers," said Marcus.

"As you wish, sir. I will have both sent here later this afternoon," said the doctor. "Is there anything else?"

"No, that will do, and thank you, Timotheus."

The doctor saluted and left. Marcus contemplated the bread and oil and decided that even after his discussion about poisons, he was a little hungry after all.

X

Marcus contemplated the mound of luggage piled on the Tarraco pier. "Taking the whole Legion with us, are we, sir?" asked Flavius, looking over the vast pile of boxes, chests, bags, and satchels that stood higher than the two men and spread a good 20 feet in all directions. Slaves were already moving some of the baggage to the ship tied up at the dock. Demaratus joined the two men.

"What is that thing?" asked Flavius nodding toward a high hulled, single-masted ship that took up much of the dock.

"It is a corbita, sir, normally a cargo vessel for shipping grain and large numbers of passengers."

"Where are the oars?" asked Marcus.

"No oars, sir. She carries a large sail on that mast. A corbita can carry a lot, but she is not in a hurry to get anyplace. Normally it would take six days to sail from Tarraco to Ostia, but we should probably add a day and half extra with this ship."

Marcus flinched internally, although he was hoping that the doctor's poppy mixture would spare him the worst of his sea sickness.

Aelia had rented the ship and turned it into a floating domus, with colorful tents covering much of the deck. Demaratus cast a critical eye on the layout and muttered something about the wind and the tents and rocky shores. Asked to elucidate by Flavius, the signifer declined. "It is best not to draw the gods' attention, sir. What one says out loud can come to pass," he said.

The comment surprised Flavius, who thought of the Greek as someone not particularly impressed with gods. But that was Demaratus on land. The powerful and arbitrary nature of the sea can easily turn the rational into the superstitious. Reminded of the dangers, Flavius looked around the dockside, searching for the augures he had arranged for.

A large carpentum, with iron-clad wheels and a high, arched roof, was making its way down the dock, pulled by several slaves. Marcus suspected it contained Aelia and Rachel. Coventina had come by foot with Demaratus, although they had rented a small, two-wheeled cart to carry their luggage. The tall Celt was unloading it now. When a slave stepped up to help her, she waved him off.

The big carpentum came to a halt and a slave opened the door. Out stepped Aelia—looking radiant—followed by Rachel, who appeared subdued. Marcus wondered what that was about. As always, Aelia took over, lightly kissing Marcus on the cheek, greeting Flavius and Demaratus, waving at Coventina, and directing where she wanted certain pieces of luggage to go on the ship. Marcus sighed. He was in love with this woman, but she had the ability to make one feel like a piece of furniture.

Aelia had boarded the ship and was met by what Marcus

assumed to be the captain. The two huddled aft by the steering oar, deep in conversation.

"Sir?" said Flavius, indicating the two augures approaching the ship and carrying a chicken.

"Right," said Marcus, "Let's look to our future." He actually did not much believe in the predictions of priests—the gods were on the side of the big legions—but he knew his optio thought highly of them.

The augures, accompanied by a soldier carrying a spear, approached and greeted Marcus and Flavius. The priests were attached to the VII Legion and had performed this ritual on countless occasions. One augure held the chicken, while the other scattered a handful of grain. The chicken was set down— the bird also knew the drill—and began pecking away at the grain, while both priests observed him closely. The chicken made short work of the grain, then began strutting, cocking its head and generally moving around with the locomotion of his tribe.

Coventina had come to watch, joined by Rachel.

"What are they doing?" whispered Coventina to Demaratus, "and who is that soldier?"

"It's a sacred chicken, and the way it pecks predicts the future," he said, "The soldier is a pullator."

"Chickens are sacred?" said the Celt. "I like them with olive oil and rosemary. It never occurred to me that I was eating a god."

Demaratus tried to shush her as Flavius shot an annoyed glance in their direction. "The chickens are not gods, they merely tell us the gods' intentions," he whispered back. "As for the soldier, I really don't know. It is just the way it is done.

"Chickens. Did you know our future depends on chickens, Rachel?" Coventina whispered.

Rachel suppressed a smile. She was aware that Flavius looked dead serious about the business. "It is best we remain quiet, Coventina," she whispered back.

Coventina muttered, "And they call us barbarians?" but then went silent.

An augure picked up the chicken and turned to Marcus. "We foresee a safe passage to your destination, legate," he said.

"What about beyond that?" asked Flavius.

"We can see the immediate future, optio, but you will need to consult our brotherhood when you arrive at your destination to further divine what the gods have in store for you," he said.

"Good work if you can get it," whispered Coventina.

"Really, my love, you must learn to curb that tongue of yours," whispered Demaratus.

She gave him a considered look. "Many have tried that with my people," she whispered back, "but none have succeeded." With that she left and returned to the luggage, lifted two large bags and headed for the gangway.

The two augures had brought out small statues of Oceanus, God of the seas, and his companion, Tethys. They began chanting a prayer, while Flavius looked on. Demaratus left to help Coventina, but Rachel held back, waiting for Flavius.

When the priests had finished, they gathered up the statues and Flavius handed them a small purse. Rachel again suppressed a smile, "Good work if you can get it, indeed," she thought. She was developing a real affection for Coventina.

Finally, Flavius turned and greeted her rather stiffly. "I make him awkward," thought Rachel, which she considered rather sweet. "Would you help me, Flavius?" she asked, knowing that her request would put him more at ease.

He smiled broadly. "Of course, Rachel. Show me what you want done."

Marcus watched all this play out. He sympathized with the Celt's sentiments—really, chickens?—and was interested in the interplay of his second-in-command and Rachel. Flavius was taken with the woman, but it was not clear the sentiment was returned. Things could get complicated, and there was nothing he could do about it. He picked up both of his bags and went aboard.

The captain—a short, rotund man with a well-trimmed beard and wearing a cap that covered his baldness—came forward to greet him.

"Honor to you, Legate Marcus Favonius," he said, "Tarraco is much in your debt. I am Jovinus Licinius."

Marcus shook hands with the man, and the two briefly made polite conversation. "As soon as the luggage is aboard, sir," said Jovinus, "the *Juno* will be pulled away from the quay and we will get underway." Marcus noticed two smaller ships with oars maneuvering near the ship's bow, while several crew members handled two thick ropes. He assumed they would be used to pull the ship out of the harbor. Worried as he was about sea sickness, he found the process interesting, although he couldn't imagine how oars on the two small vessels could move something as large as the *Juno*.

What with the tents and luggage, there was not a lot of room on the deck, and most of the luggage was being moved below.

The captain had broken off the conversation to oversee the stowage, and Marcus drifted over to watch. There were several open hatches, and slaves were carrying luggage and supplies down ladders as the captain directed them where to place things.

"What are they doing?" he asked Demaratus, who had appeared at his side to watch the storage.

"Ballast, sir," answered the signifer.

"Ballast?" asked Marcus.

"Placement of ballast is important, sir," said Demaratus.

"Why?" asked Marcus.

"The ship must be correctly balanced, sir. One normally does that with rocks and cargo. In our case, we have a lot of luggage. If a ship is out of balance, she could capsize," he answered.

Marcus nodded. "Your former world, signifer."

"Yes, sir," agreed Demaratus, looked pained. Marcus was certain the Greek did not approve of the way this "ballast" was being placed. His signifer thought that in matters nautical the Romans were the very definition of incompetent. Then again, he had watched Demaratus step in and take over a ship in the middle of a storm that might well have killed them all had he not intervened. He also had seen Demaratus take a fleet of ships out to sea and then land them exactly where he wanted them to be. When it came to ships, the Greek knew what he was talking about.

With Demaratus caught up in watching the *Juno* being stowed and Flavius in conversation with Rachel near one of the tents, Marcus discreetly moved to the ship's bow and slipped a silver flask out of his cloak. Following the doctor's order, he shook it vigorously and downed a mouthful. The poppy juice had a bitter aftertaste, and after a few moments his mouth began to numb.

* * *

Preparing for their departure drew Marcus's thoughts to the coming reunion with his family, about which he had very mixed feelings. He did not remember his youth with great fondness. His father had encouraged competition between his two older brothers, Tiberius and Mamercus, and largely ignored him and his sister, Julia. Marcus had always thought it a cruel strategy for raising children, since primogeniture guaranteed that the younger, Mamercus, could never win. Not that he didn't try, generally by pushing limits. In the end it would lead him to challenge the Praetorians and to his own death at the hands of the Guard.

Marcus and Julia watched this sibling rivalry from a distance. The older brothers either paid them no attention or bullied them. Julia coped by marrying young and fleeing the family, an unfortunate choice, in Marcus's opinion, because she ended up with a foolish and not overly bright husband. On the other hand, she had produced a charming and intelligent daughter, Sabina, with whom Marcus had been corresponding for the past year.

His way out was to join the army. At first it felt like exile, but over the years he had developed a fondness for the order it brought to his life, and he did well, sometimes even surprising himself. His rise from a junior tesserarius to centurion was all of his own making. His efficiency as a third-in-command led to his appointment as optio of his century, and his elevation to centurion was earned on the battlefield. During a desperate battle in Britannia, he had been awarded a Corona Vallarius for leading his men over the walls of an Ordovician hill fort. The first man who followed him over that wall—and likely saved his life that day by holding off a counterattack—was Flavius. When Marcus was awarded the Corona and elevated to centurion, he appointed Flavius his optio, and the two had been inseparable ever since.

Now he was returning home. To what? Mamercus was dead, and Tiberius was maneuvering in the current power vacuum that always follows in the wake of a new emperor. He was anxious to see Julia and Sabina, less so his elder brother. Here he was, an acting legate, the hero of the siege of Tarraco, and he was fretting over what his family thought about him. Status and accomplishment faded when confronted with the intricacies of family life. In Hispania he was honored and obeyed, in his family he was just the younger brother of little consequence.

All in all, the reunion promised to be complex.

He was feeling a little sorry for himself. As a legion commander without a legion, he really had nothing to contribute to the preparations for a sea voyage. Finding a deserted spot at the ship's starboard, he made himself inconspicuous. The luggage was aboard, the captain had retreated to the stern to be near the steering oar, and slaves were loosening the bolster ropes tying the ship to the wharf. The two smaller boats had attached ropes to their sterns, and the rowers were digging in with their oars. Slowly the huge *Juno* moved away from the dock toward the center of the harbor as sailors began raising an enormous square sail on the mast.

Marcus found it all fascinating. He had never paid much

attention to the way that ships worked, largely because he was either distracted by apprehension about getting sick or deep in the clutches of nausea. But the poppies were making him lightheaded and feeling rather good.

The sail billowed and the ship heeled over to port and began maneuvering toward the harbor entrance. The two tugs had cast off their lines and were moving out of the way of the *Juno*. The big ship cleared the entrance, rolling and heaving as her bow met the seas. Marcus took a deep breath, but soon relaxed. He was feeling quite pleasant and not sick at all. He was also a little dizzy. Might he have taken too deep a swallow?

Aelia loomed above him, looking a little concerned. "How are you, Marcus?" she asked.

He gave her a broad smile. "Fine, my dear."

She smiled back. "You might want to see your quarters. Flavius has taken your things into one of the tents, and we are unpacking."

"I will be along in a few moments, Aelia," he replied. "I find the view most interesting."

She smiled, hugged him and left, thinking, "May the gods bless the good doctor and his medicine."

XI

The four men stretched out on couches around a marble table in a room lit with a dozen or more oil lamps. Frescos, featuring wild life and plants, covered the walls and ceiling. Three of the men were dressed in the toga of senators, a narrow purple stripe bordering the garment's edges. Two had cast off their senatorial shoes—black leather with a crescent decorating the top—and loosened their undergarments. The meal had been heavy, featuring a "Trojan pig"—a suckling stuffed with a variety of meats— a sow's udder filled with African snails, and several vegetable dishes, topped off with a dulcia domestica of dates, dried fruits, nuts, cake crumbs and spices soaked in wine. Julius Dasumi's toga was no less rich than those of the three senators, but he lacked that much-desired stripe.

"It does not seem overly complex to me, gentlemen," he said. "The will violates Roman law and is an abomination that threatens every man in the Empire."

Publius Acilius, the senior senator—thin, with a full head of silver hair, and the oldest by a decade—took a sip of his wine.

"Law is what the emperor wills it, Julius. We are not the Senate of the Republic."

"Indeed," put in Lucius Minicius—a heavy man, bordering on corpulent, and bald as an egg, "there are 600 of us, and yet we have less power than we did when our membership was a mere 300. There is no argument with it being repugnant for a woman to inherit equally, but you want us to reverse a decision by an emperor endorsed by the Senate. That is a lot to ask."

"An emperor who is dead," said Julius bluntly.

"But an emperor, nonetheless," interjected Avidius Cassius. "Do not speak ill of him." Avidius, the youngest of the senators, was not a Patrician, and he was the only one of the four who had served in the Army, mostly in Gaul.

"That is dangerous talk, Julius," said Publius softly, leaning back on his couch and holding up his glass. A slave immediately filled it from an ornate pitcher. "Speaking of dead emperors is slippery ground. Many of them have ended up in that state in recent years, including the late unlamented Philip."

"Gentleman, we digress from the matter at hand," protested Julius, an impatient edge to his voice.

Lucius let out a belch. "I think you are not taking into account our priorities at this time, Julius." A slave refilled his glass. "The Emperor Decius—may divine Augusta watch over him—is still consolidating his rule. There is trouble on the Dacian border where the Goths grow arrogant, and Gaul is restive."

Avidius nodded. "More than restive," he said. "They tire of Roma taking their tax money and giving little in return."

"Enough of that," said Publius sharply. "We should address the will of Julius and his sister."

"But we cannot do that without talking about the larger situation," argued Lucius. "We have a new emperor who is still in the process of lining up support. Gaul is relevant because Decius needs its support." Turning to look directly at Julius, he added, "Decius will do what is in his own interests, and the traditions of Roman law are not high on his agenda. The commander of the VII Legion that defeated the Franks is a Favonius, the brother of Tiberius Favonius, who is not only a strong supporter of Decius, he was so when it was dangerous. Decius will not forget that. Nor that another Favonius brother was killed by the Praetorian Guard at the order of the Arab."

"The Favonius drew his sword and was killed only after he had struck down one of the Praetorians," Publius objected. "He was not executed. And no emperor is going to challenge the Guard, particularly since it remained neutral in the fight between the Arab and Decius."

"What is your point, Publius?" asked Julius, his exasperation evident.

"My point is that a will between you and your sister is not going to loom large on the emperor's agenda. It will be decided not on the basis of what is law, but what is good for Decius," answered the senior senator.

"In short, gold," said Julius cynically.

"Gold is always a good idea," agreed Publius. "There are many senators who borrowed money to secure a seat, and that money needs to be repaid."

"I think I can be helpful there," said Julius. "I just need some names."

"But even if a majority of senators agree with you, Julius,

you will need the emperor to endorse it. That won't be so easy," said Avidius. "And in the end, it must pass through the Vestal Virgins."

"I thought that was pro forma," said Julius. "If the Senate and the emperor want it, the Virgins will go along."

Publius shrugged. "These are not normal times, and the Virgins are jealous of their power. There are many pieces to this puzzle, Julius, and you'll need them to be in alignment."

Julius's face tightened with frustration, but he reined it in. "How should I proceed?" he asked.

There was a long silence.

"Well, if something bad happened to your sister that would make this all easy," said Lucius. The other two senators looked uncomfortable but said nothing.

"Accidents do happen," said Julius. "And Roma is a dangerous city."

"Indeed," said Publius, "but that is not a matter for us. If you want our help, we need gold," he said bluntly.

"And you will have it, Publius," replied Julius.

"Then let us drink to the rule of law," said Avidius. The four men drained their glasses, and the slave refilled them.

Julius waved him off. "I must leave you, senators. I have much to do." He arose, and a slave immediately fetched him his cloak. As he was getting ready to leave, the slave pulled at his sleeve. "Sir, this is for you," he said, as he handed him a folded piece of papyrus. Julius slipped it into his sleeve and went out to a waiting litter chair. It was held by four slaves accompanied by two burly body guards who took their place at the rear of the litter.

* * *

As the outer door closed, Publius turned to the others. "Your thoughts?"

Lucius shrugged. "This will be costly," he said. "And we will need more information. We do not want to antagonize the new emperor."

"Yes, to both," agreed Publius. He turned to Avidius. "Senator, you must be careful of what you say, and, most importantly, you must not speak of Gaul. That is a most sensitive subject, and we need to avoid being associated with it. That would be treason."

"How do we avoid it?" asked Avidius. "The Favonius who commanded the VII Legion certainly knows that the Gaul legions allowed the Franks to pass unmolested, and it takes no great intelligence to figure out that something big is afoot. It is only a matter of time before this Marcus asks difficult questions. Some of those questions may come uncomfortably close to the three of us."

Publius nodded. "If something were to happen to him as well, that would be helpful."

"That may come to pass," Avidius put in.

Publius arched an eyebrow. "What do you mean?"

"My sources in the Guard tell me that the Praetorians have not dropped their animosity toward this Favonius from Hispania. They may solve our problem for us," he said. "As we all know, Roma can be a dangerous place."

XII

Marcus thought he had never seen anything quite as wonderful as the low, black bar on the horizon—the coast of Italia. He gripped the side of the ship and said a short prayer to Carna, the god that protects people's health. The doctor's poppy formula had worked for the first four days of the voyage, but he had not rationed the potion correctly, and on the night of the fourth day the flask had run dry. Within hours he began feeling queasy, and by morning he was in the full throes of sea sickness. After two and a half days of misery, the end was now in sight.

It had been an odd trip. The first part was like a long picnic. Aelia had packed a wide variety of food and drink, and the tents were filled with pillows and bedding wrapped in fancy fabrics. Days were spent conversing and watching dolphins, evenings in eating and drinking.

It was typical of Aelia's general approach to life. A serious business was always made lighter by a good party. However, Marcos knew that her festive approach to the voyage masked her deep unease about its potential outcome. In a very real way, her life—or life as Aelia defined it—was at stake.

Flavius, Demaratus and Coventina had been careful, because the lines of class and caste were blurred in the confines of the ship. The three tended to hang back and watch more than actively participate, They'd been polite but guarded. Flavius seemed distracted, Demaratus protective of a somewhat distant Coventina, and Rachel subdued, which made Aelia all the more energetic in her efforts to keep the conversation lively. All in all, the company was enjoyable but exhausting.

At various points during the trip, Demaratus and Flavius went into a huddle, and Marcus wondered what they were about. At least, he had wondered for the first part of the trip. Once his malady struck, the only thing that he wondered about was if he was going to die, and whether that was not such a bad idea.

* * *

"I am not sure what to make of it," said Flavius, "she just isn't very friendly."

"I don't think she is being unfriendly, comrade, I think something is bothering her," said Demaratus.

"Maybe me," the optio said gloomily.

"Didn't you have a conversation with her at the beginning of the trip?" asked the signifer. "She looked like she was interested in talking to you."

Flavius nodded. "Yes, we talked about the trip, and she joked about all the luggage Aelia was bringing with her."

"Joked?" asked Demaratus.

"Well, it was said as a joke, but she didn't seem to approve," admitted Flavius.

"I think that may be the problem," said Demaratus. "Aelia

adopted Rachel as a sister, but we both know that one is wealthy and influential and the other a former slave. That cannot be an easy fit."

"You think?" asked Flavius with a note of hope. "Have you made an effort to contact Aelia about Rachel?"

Demaratus felt a stab of guilt. He had told Flavius that he would act as an intermediary with Rachel and talk with Aelia about the matter, but the Frankish invasion and its aftermath had intervened. He had spent several weeks establishing his household with Coventina and had put his promise aside.

"I have not," admitted the signifer, "and that would seem to be a fortunate turn of events."

"How so?" asked Flavius narrowing his eyes.

"If I am correct—and your initial conversations with Rachel suggest she is not being unfriendly, only distracted—then enlisting Aelia may not be a good idea at this point. Aelia may be part of the problem, Flavius. I suggest an alternative approach."

"What?" asked Flavius, looking suspicious.

"If Rachel is feeling like an outsider, then we need another outsider to figure that out," answered Demaratus.

"Who?"

"Coventina," answered Demaratus. "She is not a Roman, and she is certainly not wealthy. And a conversation between two women about men is perfectly normal. It is certainly not one I can have with Rachel."

Flavius stared at the sea and was quiet for a long time. He finally said, "I see your logic, but I am not comfortable with a lot of people knowing about how I feel."

"That is an understatement," thought the signifer, careful

not to voice that observation. "Let me talk with Coventina and see if she is willing to have a conversation with Rachel," said Demaratus.

Flavius nodded reluctantly.

* * *

Rachel watched the flying fish skimming alongside the *Juno*, the sunlight flashing off their scales. She was struggling with her feelings and unclear what to do about them. She genuinely loved Aelia, but this trip was a perfect encapsulation of what bothered her. The level of luxury was beyond anything she had experienced before, and Rachel had been a household slave for a prosperous family. She knew Aelia was not trying to be conspicuous. Indeed, she was probably unconscious about the cost of renting a whole ship and stocking it with the best of food and drink. Her adopted sister was not a snob, nor did she look down on those who were not of her wealth or status. In fact, one of Aelia's genuine charms is that she did not really care about class. Of course, that was also a luxury of wealth. The really rich could afford to act like everyday people.

But she knew she was also being unfair. Aelia was the exact opposite of most upper-class women. During their time together as slaves, she had shown great courage and a willingness to sacrifice for others. She was intelligent, funny, and a great companion. She also was in love with a very decent man, who had gathered to him some impressive friends. That line of thinking led her back to Flavius. She felt a pang of guilt. Flavius had been welcoming and friendly at the beginning of the voyage, but she had been so wrapped up in her own preoccupations that she had not reciprocated. She liked Flavius and she certainly did not want to make him feel bad, and he had looked glum for the past few days. She really must get ahold of herself.

With that thought, she willed herself into a better mood—it was a trick slaves were good at—and turned back to the tents. She saw Flavius look in her direction, and she smiled and gave him a little wave. He smiled and waved back.

* * *

Ever since it became obvious that Marcus had run out of seasickness medicine, Aelia had been willing the ship to move faster. She felt sorry for him, but she was also a little annoyed. Why couldn't men take care of themselves? She would make sure to bring a backup supply of the poppy syrup for the return voyage.

But a seasick lover was not her main concern. She knew her brother was a dangerous foe. He had had several weeks to poison the well and recruit allies in his campaign to overthrow their father's will. But she had resources of her own. She would need them all.

* * *

The ship arrived in the early morning. The fire in the lighthouse was burning down, and the keepers were adjusting the huge mirror to mark the port's location for daylight ships. A statue of Portunus, the god of harbors, sat opposite the lighthouse at the end of a long mole enclosing the south flank of the port.

The crew dropped the huge main sail, and a cluster of small

boats maneuvered her to the dock. Then began the long process of dragging the luggage out of the hold and moving it to land, with Aelia and Rachel directing the operation as if they were maneuvering a century in battle.

XIII

"Report," said Antonius Clodius. The Praetorian tribune sat behind a small desk piled with scrolls and wax tablets. A cup of wine sat undrunk at his elbow. It had been a long day and he was tired, but he hid it well. "Never show weakness"—if there was a Praetorian Guard slogan, that was it.

Aulus Nonius, his aide, cleared his throat. "The acting legate of the VII Legion Hispania, Marcus Favonius, along with his second- and third-in-command, arrived yesterday in the port of Ostia, sir. He is accompanying the sister of Julius Dasumi and two other women I have no information on."

"Impressive, Aulus," replied the tribune. "I commend your speed in this matter. How did you do it?"

"I contacted several former members of the Guard who currently reside in Hispania, in particular those who live in port cities on the province's east coast, the most likely place Favonius would choose for a voyage to the capitol," the clerk replied. "I asked them to keep track of ships headed for Roma. A lucky circumstance did the rest."

The tribune raised an eyebrow, "And that was?"

"The story of Favonius and this Aelia Dasumi is well known in Hispania. The only thing that travels faster than a man on horseback is gossip. A former member of the Guard who happened to be in a harborside café overheard a sea captain talking about renting out his ship to this Dasumi woman, who wanted it to take her party to Roma," Aulus continued. "He waited a day and then went to the docks and asked the captain what he charged for carrying passengers to Roma. The captain told him his ship was already rented and restricted to one party. During their conversation, the captain mentioned the date he was to carry the party to Ostia. Our man immediately sent a letter by a small trading vessel, paying its captain a generous fee to make sure it was delivered to our headquarters."

"That is an intelligent and enterprising man," said Antonius. "I assume your repayment was generous?"

"Yes, sir, and in gold."

"Any word on where Favonius is staying during his time here?" asked the Tribune.

"No, sir. I assume with his brother or his sister. I have men watching both houses," replied Aulus.

"And the Dasumi brother?"

"We are watching him. He is meeting with senators and, we assume, offering them bribes." The clerk was silent a moment, then added, "There is an aspect of this I have only just become aware of, sir."

"What?" asked Antonius.

"Julius Dasumi is currently under a cloud, sir," replied Aulus. "Some of the Tarraco authorities have accused him of collaborating with the Franks when they controlled the city. He denies it and says he only helped set up a market so that people could find food. Some say the prices were usurious, and the market eventually set off a riot."

"Is the charge valid?" asked Antonius.

Aulus hesitated. "I don't have really solid information on that, sir. Some say yes, others say no. I think it is unclear. If you like I can pursue it further."

"No need," said the tribune, "continue."

The clerk went on, "He is extremely wealthy, but I think we should be careful what kind of contact we make with him."

The Tribune considered this for a moment. "Agreed, but keep a watch on him. He might be useful."

"Yes, sir. We have him under surveillance."

Antonius paced the room for a moment, thinking." You have done an outstanding job, Aulus, and you can be certain that the legate will know about this."

"My duty, sir," replied the clerk.

"Many do their duty, Aulus, not so many do it well," the Tribune said. "Keep me informed."

The clerk knew when he was being dismissed. He saluted and closed the door behind him.

The Tribune rocked back and forth on his heels. There were many moving parts in this situation. The Favonius family and the new emperor. The legion commander who was likely responsible for the death of two Praetorians. The Dasumi brother and sister fighting over a will. All those pieces were converging on the board. He smiled to himself. This was like a game, and Antonius Clodius enjoyed games.

The tribune pushed himself away from his desk and began

pacing. His office was spacious, the second largest in the Principia. Only the Legion's legate's office was larger. This mattered to Antonius, who liked the trappings of power.

The source of that power lay in the rule that the Guard was the only legion allowed in Roma. Well, that and the fact that the Praetorians were also twice the size of a regular army legion.

The Principia was set in the middle of the Legion's huge camp in the Campus Martius, in the very heart of the Empire's capital. In addition to the 11,000 legionnaires, the camp housed the army of clerks and aides that kept the organization functioning.

The tribune was well aware that the Praetorians' extra pay and privileges were not popular with the rest of the army, and he suspected that the legionnaires were not particularly discomforted by the deaths of a few Guard members. Indeed, they probably cheered it.

Which is why the Guard needed to maintain its reputation for ruthlessness. Antonius knew that reputation was, in part, a sham. The Praetorians kept their privilege and position by being adept at politics. You can do a lot of things with swords, but you can't sit on them. To maintain power requires one to build alliances, find common ground, and convince your opponents that it is in their interest to compromise. This is what the tribune had to think through. What was in the interest of the Praetorian Guard in this matter? Sometimes revenge was required, but revenge for its own sake was self-indulgent and could do more harm than good.

XIV

The *Juno* was docked in the outer Harbor of Claudius, the only option given that a vessel of her size had difficulty negotiating her way into the inner Trajan Harbor. The luggage was being taken off and loaded onto a barge. Aelia had arranged for the party and their belongings to travel by boat up the Tiber to the center of the city. The barge—or barges, since there were two, one for people, the other for luggage—would be pulled by oxen, an additional expense, but one that Aelia could easily cover. The distance was not great—less than a day's march by a legion—but then a legion traveled lighter.

Flavius and Demaratus saw to Marcus's luggage, because the man was still too sick to do more than sit quietly and breathe deeply. At least he was no longer vomiting, not that he had anything left to throw up. He was also feeling the effects of the poppy syrup on his innards, which had largely ceased to function. Miserable was an understatement. He quietly vowed that under no circumstance would he return to Hispania by boat.

Flavius appeared at his elbow. "Sir, we need to board the barges." The optio tried to make light conversation about how different their current situation was from the last time the three men had been at the harbor. "We were on the run then," he said with a chuckle, "Now we have a fancy barge to take us to Roma."

A bad-tempered glare from Marcus silenced him.

But eventually Marcus began feeling better, even lightheaded —although that was partly due a to lack of food—and made his way to the passenger barge. Everyone was careful to avoid looking at him, which only put him in a fouler mood. Aelia brought him a cup of wine and some fresh bread. He initially recoiled, but after a sip and a mouthful, he felt marginally better. He was not ready for conversation, but he had rejoined the human race.

The barge was comfortable and the day warm. Roma had not yet descended into the clinging mugginess of summer, and Marcus dozed on and off. Aelia was busy organizing luggage, pointing out to crew members where she wanted them to place bags. Some would accompany them on their barge, the rest would follow on the other.

"I understand we are to stay at Marcus's sister's," said the signifer.

Flavius nodded. "Her name is Julia Aquillius, and she has a pack of kids. Two boys and a girl. Julia is okay. Her husband is Lucius." The optio shrugged. "Not the quickest calf in the pasture."

"Will they be able to handle all of our party?" asked Demaratus.

"Oh, they have a large domus, but I can't see Aelia being very comfortable there. I am sure Aelia has something grander in mind," said Flavius.

Demaratus leaned back against the stern rail. "We need to

stay together, comrade. I doubt our arrival will go unnoticed," he cautioned.

Flavius nodded. "The Guard has an ear to the ground. They will know that we are here."

"What about your family?" asked Demaratus.

"I will go visit them after we get settled in," said Flavius. "They will help me contact my cousins for a little help with our security."

"What of your cousin in the Guard?" asked the signifer.

Flavius hesitated. "I am not sure about Titus," he said finally. "The Praetorians knew where we were, Demaratus. They sent those assassins after us. The only other person who knew that was Titus. He knew I was going to the vigils because our former commander from Britannia, Quintus Pompeius, was legate."

"He might not have given that information freely," said Demaratus.

"No, he might not have, but I suspect he didn't try very hard to hide our tracks. I don't really blame him. And, after all, he did warn us that the Guard was after us." Flavius paused. "I will have to be careful with that one," he said finally.

"Careful is what we all need to be, brother," said Demaratus.

Flavius nodded and changed the subject. "Did you speak with your woman about Rachel?"

"I did and she is willing to have that conversation," answered Demaratus. "I did notice that Rachel seemed friendlier."

Flavius sighed. "She is, and I found out what is bothering her, although we need to keep this between the two of us."

Demaratus cocked an eyebrow.

"It's delicate," said Flavius. This was not a word Demaratus had ever expected to hear from the optio. "Rachel is uncomfortable with the kind of wealth that is second nature to Aelia. She bears Aelia no animus, but it is not the life she is used to. She doesn't know what to do with her feelings about this."

"She had this conversation with you?" asked Demaratus.

"Yes. Is that a problem?" replied Flavius.

"There is no problem, brother. But if she is talking with you about a subject like this, that is very good news."

"I guess," said Flavius, folding his arms and looking down at the deck.

"Flavius, do you remember the conversation we had just before we heard the news of the Franks taking Tarraco?" asked Demaratus.

Flavius nodded.

"And that I said you had one problem when it came to women?" pressed Demaratus.

Again, Flavius nodded. "You said women might mistake my wariness as a lack of interest."

"Exactly. So, not a 'guess.' Rachel is confiding in you. She would only do that with someone she likes and trusts," said Demaratus.

Flavius nodded. "Hmm."

Demaratus squeezed his shoulder and left to stand by Coventina. Flavius relaxed a little. The day seemed brighter. It got still brighter when Rachel wandered over to him and asked, "What are those?" pointing at several boats being loaded with grain sacks.

"Naves codicariae," he answered. "Probably unloaded at Portus after a voyage from Egypt or Mauretania."

"Are they going to Roma?" she asked.

He nodded. "Pulled by slaves, mostly. Oxen are a luxury. It's hard work against the current."

Rachel could see several boats further up the Tiber being hauled by teams of slaves. The boats had masts that were struck down to the deck, with a helmsman at the side rudder to keep each ship in a straight line. "Slaves are cheaper than oxen," she said softly. Flavius glanced at her but said nothing. Slavery was a delicate issue around Rachel. "Thank you, Flavius," she said, patting his arm before wandering over to join Coventina, who was standing at a rail.

The issue of slavery made Flavius uncomfortable. It brought him back to the time two years before when the century was leaving Corduba headed for Legio. An execution had held up the unit's progress, and Flavius had gone to straighten out the situation. The local vigils were crucifying an entire household of slaves because one among them had killed their master. The condemned included a young child whom Flavius had killed to save her from the torture of a slow death. He had suppressed the image, but at times like this it came to his mind unbidden.

He did not want to think about slavery, yet there was the fact that Rachel had been a slave. Was she abused? Was she—and at this thought his mind reeled—raped? Ever since freeing Rachel and Aelia from the Mauri slavers, Flavius had become more aware of slaves, people he had paid no attention to in the past. When he saw one being beaten or one who looked particularly abused, he thought of Rachel. He found it deeply disconcerting and did his best to think of other things.

* * *

Rachel and Coventina—provincial tourists in the heart of Empire— watched the countryside go by. At one point Rachel went over to where Aelia was organizing their belongings, only to be waved away. "Go watch the scenery, especially the city when we come to it," said Aelia. So, Rachel returned to Coventina's side.

It was a pleasant journey, the countryside slowly giving over to the outskirts of the city. Two huge aqueducts, which Flavius identified as the Aqua Cladia and the Aqua Marcia, swept across the land and into the city. Demaratus joined the group. Eventually a large structure loomed up to starboard. Rachel pointed at the structure and asked, "What is that, Flavius?"

"The Circus Maximus," he replied. "We're landing at the Forum of Boarium, which is also the cattle market. At that, the two women wrinkled their noses.

The barge slid alongside a wharf. It was late afternoon by the time the barges tied up at the Portus Aemila. The Capitoline Hill rose up to the east, with Trajan's Forum wedged between it and the Palatine Hill, with its temples and palaces. To the south was the enormous Circus.

Coventina and Rachel were riveted. It was a city of marble built to overawe, the seat of an empire that ran from the windswept moors of northern Britannia to the deserts of southern Egypt, from the trading cities of the Pontus Euxinos, the wealthy centers of the Levant, and the oasis-dotted coast of Mauretania.

For Flavius and Marcus, it was home, and the familiar smells and the thronging crowds tugged at their memories.

Marcus—almost recovered from his ordeal—negotiated for two enclosed carpenti for the passengers and two hand-pulled carts for their baggage. He was pressed for time because no one wanted to be out in Roma at night, and the light was beginning to fade. They were not far from his sister's domus, but Roma traffic was dense and chaotic.

Julia's domus was on the slopes of the Quirinal Hill, no great distance, but getting there took them through the heart of the city. Marcus masked his impatience at delays—what essential luggage to take with them, a change of clothes and the valuables —and how to divide the party. He settled upon having Aelia, Rachel and Marcus in one carpentum and Flavius, Demaratus and Coventina in the other.

Marcus took Flavius and Demaratus aside. "Put yourselves by the door of the carpentum and loosen your swords. I don't expect trouble, but if it comes, the door is the most defensible place to be." Both nodded.

Flavius suggested that he and Demaratus accompany the carts on foot, but Marcus vetoed that. "A man on foot in a crowd is vulnerable," he pointed out. "And we may not be the target of an attack. The Praetorians are not the only ones who wish us harm. The easiest way for Julius to win his case is to kill his sister." Both men nodded. "We will make sure that doesn't happen, sir," said Flavius.

When everything was finally settled, their baggage stowed on the covered carts, the party got underway, threading its way through the crowded streets filled with merchants, shoppers, slaves on errands and people hawking everything from food to pigeons. The carpenti had windows on both sides, and Rachel and Coventina moved back and forth from one to the other, taking in the combination of grandeur and grunge—temples glowing with marble and ramshackle insulae, wealthy patricians borne on decorated litters, mingling with shoppers, teams of slaves, and beggars. There was even a snake charmer. Flavius explained to Coventina that it really was a poisonous snake, but its fangs and poison sacks had been removed. "It's for the provincials," he said.

"I'm a provincial," the Celt pointed out.

"Right you are," laughed Flavius. "You'll see lots of strange things in this city."

* * *

Eventually the carpenti arrived, and the party dragged themselves into Marcus's sister's domus—to Coventina, almost a palace, to Aelia, a modest, middle-class house—and there was a slight reduction of the chaos. It was quieter than the street, but there were family hugs and kisses and formal introductions. Julia's eyes widened at Aelia's dress and jewelry, even though the latter was wearing what was for her the bare minimum. The children stayed in the background, although Marcus gave Sabina a special embrace and said they would get a chance to speak the next day. Everyone yearned for a bath, but the public ones were closed this late in the evening, so a quick washup would have to do.

It had been a very long day at the end of a very long voyage.

XV

Julius Dasumi was impatient. The meeting with the senators had not gone well. It was obvious to him that none of them wanted to do anything precipitous. They were waiting to get a feel for the new emperor, and Decius seemed to be focused on only two things these days—Goths and Christians. The former were crossing the Dacian border, and, according to the senators, towns and cities all over Dacia were clamoring for legions to defend them.

The state's treasury, however, was thin. It cost money to keep a legion in the field, and since the Goths were coming in strength, Roma's normal expenses were multiplied three- or fourfold. It also was springtime, so shipments of grain were only starting to trickle in. The large-scale trade in cotton, silks, incense and precious stones—with their lucrative taxes—had only just resumed. Few merchants were willing to risk their goods on the winter seas. In short, the Empire was straining to meet its costs.

As for the Christians, Julius had a difficult time figuring what that was about. The sect could be annoying, but they were hardly a threat to the Empire. Decius, however, was arresting bishops and priests, and there was even talk of public executions. To Julius it made no sense. In the little time he had spent in Roma, it was clear that the average city dweller was not interested in Christianity, but they did sympathize with those under arrest. Why create martyrs? Julius shook his head. Decius seemed to be an emperor who didn't have his priorities straight.

Julius paced outside the huge Baths of Diocletion, waiting for his contact. Senator Aridius Cassius had told him that Gnaeus Domitius was a man who got things done with discretion. But Julius had no description of the man. He had sent Gnaeus a letter on his arrival, and two days later he'd received a note instructing him to wait by the Baths and wear a green cloak over his toga. Now the man was late, the day was warm, and Julius was sweating under his cloak.

He was getting ready to leave when a non-descript man appeared before him. Dressed in a simple shirt, pants, and belt, he was someone you would pass in the street and not notice. His hair was thin, combed back without any effort to hide his growing baldness, and his only jewelry was a simple bracelet on his left wrist. Julius was ready to push by him, but the man put out an arm to stop him.

"Gnaeus?" asked Julius, not very impressed that this smallish man could be someone who "got things done."

"No names," the man said softly. "If you wish something, follow me, but at a distance."

Julius was hot, tired and annoyed. "Can't we talk here?"

The man shook his head. "Roma has many ears," he said quietly. And at that he turned abruptly and strode off.

Julius hesitated a moment, then followed. The man took a

street that threaded down the Viminal Hill, then through a cluster of three-story insulae. He turned into a narrow alley and led
the way through piles of garbage. A mangy little dog growled
and barked at him, and he kicked at it bad-temperedly, growing increasingly unhappy, not sure that he would escape being
assaulted and robbed. The man finally stepped through a door,
leaving it ajar. Julius followed.

The room was mostly bare. A rickety table and three chairs
were the sum total of furniture. There was nothing on the walls,
and the only light filtered through a broken window and the
faint glow from an oil lamp. The man took a chair and indicated
another to Julius. By this time Julius was more than annoyed. He
was not used to being treated like a commoner or walking for
long distances in the heat of the day. He was sweating and his
boots hurt. "I am not pleased," he said, shaking off his cloak and
airing out his toga. "I am a man of wealth and power and expect
to be treated as such."

The man shrugged. "You are a provincial who needs help," he
said. "Tell me what you want, and I will tell you what it will cost.
Or you can go elsewhere."

Julius mastered his temper. He was, indeed, a provincial, and
he did need help. He would have to swallow his anger or give up
on the enterprise, and that was not an option. "I need someone
eliminated," he said.

"Eliminated or killed?" asked Gnaeus. "There is a difference.
I can eliminate someone by making them disappear, generally
to a slaver, or sometimes by simply putting the fear of death
into them."

"Killed," said Julius. "I have the address where the woman is staying and her description. How much will this cost?"

"Does she have bodyguards?" asked Gnaeus.

"I suppose," answered Julius. "Her lover is a soldier and he has two soldiers with him."

Gnaeus frowned. "I cannot give you a price at this time. Give me the address and the description, and I will look into it. I will send you a note when I have seen what I am getting into and then let you know how much it will cost. Be warned, I take only gold."

"I don't see what the problem is, she is only a woman," said Julius impatiently.

"A woman who is surrounded by soldiers, Dasumi," he replied. "The Army's involvement makes things much more dangerous."

Julius signed. "All right, but I would like to get this done."

"So do it yourself," replied Gnaeus.

"I am not an assassin," said Julius angrily.

"Oh, but you are, Dasumi, just not a very courageous one," countered Gnaeus.

Julius' temper flared, but he bit his tongue. "All right," he said, controlling his tone, "I will be waiting."

The man nodded, stood and opened the door to the alley. Two hard-eyed men leaned against the wall opposite the door. "These men will see you home," said Gnaeus. "Roma can be a dangerous place."

Julius gathered his cloak and left, still seething with anger over having had to put up with Gnaeus's arrogance. But what choice did he have?

XVI

Flavius tugged at his tunic and tightened his belt. He was dressed as a civilian, in a long shirt and short pants. The only sign that he was military was his gladius sword, which he slipped under his shirt. He considered taking a light cloak, but the day was turning warm, and there was already a hint of summer mugginess in the air. He put a purse, well stocked with silver denarii and one gold aureus, inside his tunic. Everyone else in the house was either out or busy, so he quietly slipped out the front door and onto the street. Marcus and Demaratus could handle security for a few hours.

He stood near the middle of the Quirinal Hill, with the Forum of Trajan below him and the Palatine Hill overlooking it. The streets teemed with traffic that he knew would grow even denser close to the Forum. His family lived in the Campus Martius, so he turned right at the bottom of the incline, skirting the Capitoline Hill with the massive Temple of Jupiter at its crest. He had not been back in Roma for almost two years, and the smells, the noise and the throngs of people brought back memories of childhood. Flavius had no regrets about choosing

Hispania over Italia, but memories of growing up among the insulae came crowding in on him.

Hand-pulled carts carried everything from wine amphorae to marble tiles, and a myriad of shops sold clothing, shoes, and foodstuffs. A barber cut hair on the sidewalk. Small thermopolia, with street-side seats facing long counters with pots of stew, seemed to fill every corner. The smells were overwhelming: cooked food, human waste, and packed humanity sweating in the late morning warmth. For Flavius it was home, and he had a sudden stab of nostalgia that he quickly suppressed. Like the Sirens, Roma was seductive—and dangerous.

If he'd been wearing his uniform, he would have made better time. Instead of stepping aside for an officer, people jostled him, cajoled him to buy their products, or paid him no more attention than they would any other citizen going about his business. But the last thing Flavius wanted was to be noticed. He would just have to be patient.

He made his way north, the temples of Isis and Hadrian on his left, headed for a group of insulae not far from the Arch of Claudius. As he pushed his way through crowds, he reviewed what he was about. The business of hiring a couple of bodyguards was straightforward. He wanted two of his cousins, Vibius and Numerius, although they might not be available. Both were young and, as Flavius recalled, capable of handling themselves. They were a rowdy lot, but he didn't see that as a problem. What he wanted was muscle, and they had that in abundance.

Lost in thought, he almost walked past it. Home.

Well, it had not been home for a long time. Flavius had marched away north more than a decade ago. He had returned to Roma when he, Marcus, and Demaratus had fled to Hispania, but he had deliberately kept his distance from his immediate family on that visit. Close association with them might well have put them in danger from the Praetorians. The only family member whom he had contacted was his cousin, Titus Flavius, an optio in the Guard. He stopped for a moment, thinking about Titus. He hadn't decided what to do. Should he ask his family about the man, or wait until someone mentioned him? What if they didn't? He put his thoughts about Titus aside. This was not the time to deal with what his cousin had, or had not, told his Praetorian superiors.

He stood looking at the sprawling insulae where he had spent most of his younger life. Square, the three-story dwelling was constructed around an open courtyard with shops on the lower level. The timber and brick building looked a bit worn. Plaster had peeled off some walls, and the roof looked like it needed replacement. He had spent his first several years on the top floor, with no running water and no immediate access to lavatories. But with the money he had sent home from his optio pay, his father had opened a small business selling used clothing that had done quite well. The family moved down a floor, acquiring running water and with a public bathroom nearby. The Priscus family was coming up in the world, and they owed much of that to Flavius.

He was torn about his family. He didn't get along with his father, whom he experienced as rather cold and distant, and had not had contact with his younger sister, Adriana, for years. She was married to a city engineer, had three children, and lived at the other side of Roma. His mother, with whom Flavius had always been close, had kept him up on the family goings-on.

He crossed the street on the raised stones and walked through an opening into the inner courtyard festooned with laundry, packs of children racing this way and that, and knots of women gossiping. A few people glanced at him, but Flavius no longer looked like the young man who had left for the army all those years ago. He vaguely recognized some of them, but hadn't a clue as to their names. He crossed the yard and climbed up a set of stairs to his parents' door. He took a deep breath and knocked.

There was no response, so he knocked again, somewhat louder. Again, the door remained closed, and there was no sign of life within. He was turning to go when his mother, Faustina, lugging a basket of foodstuffs, came climbing up the same stairs as he had. When she got to the top, she glanced at him, then stopped and stared. "Flavius," she said, dropping the basket and reaching out her arms. "My Flavius," she repeated, tears forming at the corners of her eyes.

"Mother," he said, sweeping her up in his arms. She hugged him fiercely, murmuring, "You're home, you're home, it has been too long. So handsome. Too thin. You don't write enough." And other disjointed observations.

Flavius felt a great wave of affection. His mother looked much older, older than he had imagined, and she was heavier. Her dark hair was turning gray, and her face was tracked with wrinkles. The Priscus family was prospering, but life was hard on women, and his mother was stamped with the burdens of her sex.

She squeezed him in her arms, held his face in her hands and shook her head in disbelief. "So long, and we missed you so," she repeated several times. Finally, she pulled away and examined him. "When you left you were a boy and look at you now," she said. "You could use some pounds. I am told army food is terrible. I will fill you out."

Flavius grinned. "Don't all mothers think their children need to eat more?"

"No, not the fat ones, and not the girls, at least until they get married," she said, continuing to look him over as if he were a hare hanging in a butcher shop. "Well, come in and tell me everything," she said, hefting the basket of food and pushing the door open.

"Where is father?" asked Flavius, following her into a familiar living room that yet felt strange. By most standards, the flat was spacious. Besides the living room, which also served as a dining area, there was a small kitchen and two small cubiculi. He noticed that one of the bedrooms— he and his sister had slept there in their youth—held a loom and several piles of clothing, undoubtedly from his father's business. The furniture was simple and sparse, but his mother had decorated the walls with cloth hangings, and the couches had colorful coverings. A medium-size table and chairs pressed against the side of the living room.

"He went down by the river to see what he could pick up. Wealthy people give away their old clothes that are then sold near the Pons Aclius. Your father buys some of them, then we repair tears and worn parts and resell them," she explained, continuing to touch him and look him over. "He will be back soon. He will be so surprised."

At most times, Flavius did not like to be fussed over, but with his mother it was different. It was nice to have someone so obviously happy to see him. She also started filling him in about the family. "Your sister has wonderful children. I see them every week. They are so smart and beautiful to look at. When are you going to make me grandchildren? Why aren't you married? Why are you here? Will you be here long?" A stream of questions followed on everything from where he was stationed to his plan for life.

Flavius slowly made his way through the barrage, answering his mother's questions. Some details he kept to himself, particularly those having to do with the possible trouble with the Praetorian Guard, the matter of Aelia and the will, and the real reason why he had gone to Hispania in the first place. He told her he was not certain how long they would be in Roma, and that he was currently staying with Marcus's sister.

"Why not here, my love?" she asked. "I will clear out your old room and make it as it was when you left."

He explained that he needed to stay with his commanding officer. "We are here on official business, mother. Marcus is now the acting legate of his legion, but that appointment is not final. He needs his second-in-command with him."

"Second-in-command to a legion," she crooned, "How wonderful. That Mindius woman brags about her son, who is only a tesserarius. Wait until I tell her my Flavius is second-in-command of a legion."

"No, mother. I am Marcus's second-in-command, not of the whole legion. That would be a tribune, and I am not a tribune," Flavius tried to explain.

"And why not? You should be appointed a tribune," she said indignantly.

Flavius gave up, letting the combination of endearments and misunderstanding wash over him. It was nice to be home. His mother put out bread and fresh olive oil and dates, the latter indicating how much his family had risen from their old days on the top floor. At one point he wandered into the kitchen and marveled at the faucet. As he turned it, water streamed out. He remembered when he and Adriana had lugged amphorae down the stairs and to the communal fountain, filling and hauling them back up to the third floor.

"We wouldn't have that if it were not for you, my love," said his mother, beginning to put together the evening meal.

"Father seems to have done well," said Flavius.

"Yes, the business is a good one. People need clothing and prices are high. Good, clean garments that don't cost a week's wages are always in demand. But it was your pay that made it so," she said, slicing vegetables—onions, carrots, asparagus and beets—and tossing them into a cauldron. A small fire on the stove began to simmer the mixture, to which she eventually added ox bones, cabbage, garlic, lentils and several spoons of crushed pepper. She topped it off with coriander and tamarind. The rich aroma filled the kitchen and brought back memories of sitting around a table with his sister and parents and his mother spooning stew into his bowl. She was a good cook, and he was looking forward to supper.

Eventually his father showed up carrying a load of clothes on his back. Flavius and he embraced, although the old man—and he was indeed looking old—was stiff and somewhat formal. Flavius sighed, well that was the way of it, but he found it no longer bothered him much. "We grow up," he thought to himself, "and when we do, we put away the things of childhood."

Filled with good food and two cups of wine—better than the sour stuff he was used to in the army, but nothing like the fine wine he had been drinking for the past week—Flavius asked after the two cousins he sought.

"Humph," said his mother. "Two troublemakers, if you ask me. And working for that shark, Manius Acilius. I blame them for the death of my sister."

Now, Faustina," said his father. "Your sister died of the plague. Vibius and Numerius are not responsible for the plague."

"Who is Manius Acilius?" asked Flavius.

"Well, your mother's right about the shark part. He loans money at high interest. If you don't pay, he has a gang that goes around and explains to you why you need to come up with the money," answered Lucius.

"'Explains,'" his mother sniffed. "If by explain you mean breaking people's arms and heads."

His father shrugged. "Yes. I don't approve, but it is not my business."

"Why would you want anything to do with those two?" asked his mother. "They are nothing but trouble."

"I am not hiring them to be flamines, mother. Roma can be a dangerous place, and Marcus and his companion want to hire some bodyguards," Flavius explained.

"Well, if you want some muscle, they are your people," said his father, "but they might not come cheap."

"Cost is not a problem. I just want to know if they are reliable," he said.

"They are reliable. They are family," said his father.

"Reliable criminals are what they are," added his mother.

"Sometimes you need a thief to catch a thief, mother. And I won't need them for all that long," explained Flavius.

There was a long silence. "Well, I am sure you know what you are doing, my love. Just don't bring them around here," she finally said.

"How do I contact them?" asked Flavius.

"I know someone who knows Manius. I will say something to him tomorrow. You should leave me information as to where you are staying, and I will see if they can come around to see you," said his father. Faustina looked on disapprovingly, but said nothing.

"Thank you, father," said Flavius.

The mention of the cousins had put a temporary chill on the conversation, but Flavius gradually warmed it up with tales of what he had been doing. Even his father seemed to loosen up a little. It is possible, thought Flavius, that my father was not being cold to me. Maybe he is just an awkward person. Flavius remembered Demaratus's comment that his own lack of skill with women could be interpreted as disinterest. It was an interesting revelation and one that warmed him toward his father.

XVII

Julia, clothed in a white shift and barefooted, stepped slowly from the garden into the atrium, carefully spitting out a black bean. Her daughter, Sabina, similarly dressed and holding beans in her hand, threw one over her shoulder. Both of them passed through the living room headed for a cubiculum.

"What are they doing?" whispered Coventina, but Demaratus spread his hands and shrugged.

"It is Lemuria," said Flavius.

"And that is?" asked Coventina.

"Lemures are ghosts," explained the optio. "The beans are an offer to placate them. If you don't give them beans, they can cause trouble. Tonight is the first of three festival nights."

"Why would they cause trouble?" asked the Celt.

"Mostly lemures don't bother people, but a young lemure can be disruptive. It resents dying young," answered Flavius. "Julia may have lost a child and be worried that its ghost could prove troublesome. Roma is tough on kids."

Julia and Sabina had passed through the bedrooms and were returning to the garden. The older woman looked dead serious, even a little frightened. Her daughter appeared slightly be-mused, fluttering her fingers in a low-key greeting to Coventina, Demaratus and Flavius.

Marcus's sister let out a sigh. "Well, that's done," she said. "I will prepare dinner for us. I need your help, Sabina." Her daughter nodded dutifully, and both women disappeared into the kitchen. Moments later Rachel came through the front door with two bags full of vegetables and trailing a faint odor of fish. She, too, vanished into the kitchen.

The domus was not small, but it felt crowded with so many there. Julia and her husband had been perfect hosts, but both began looking a little frazzled after the second day. The two boys, Julius and Sergius, were noisy and boisterous, scattering their toys around the house. The adults were constantly picking their way through pottery horses on wheels and terra cotta fig-ures representing gladiators and soldiers. Sabina had her dolls, but she kept them tucked away in her room. When Marcus and Aelia arrived from their meeting with a local lawyer, the domus felt overcrowded and stifling.

Dinners were the worst. The food was decent—appetizers of eggs and fish, a main course of strongly spiced boiled meat and vegetables, and desserts of honey cakes and fruit. But the con-versation was awkward. Marcus, Flavius and Demaratus avoided talking about why they were really there, and Aelia didn't want to go into the details about the will. Rachel and Coventina were mostly silent. Julia, however, was talkative—indeed, she rarely took a breath—but most of it was shallow patter, while her husband, Lucius, had little to say. The children ate separately.

When Aelia raised the issue of moving, it was met with

obvious relief. Julia protested, but weakly. "You have been a generous and gracious host, Julia," said Aelia, "but we cannot burden you any longer. A single guest is one thing, six are an invasion."

"But where will you go?" asked Julia, the relief obvious. "Marcus's domus is even smaller than ours."

"It is indeed too small, Julia, though his pillars are quite charming. Marcus and I have made arrangements to rent a domus on the Esquiline Hill. Not only is it larger, it's also closer to where I need to be for my work," replied Aelia.

"Yes, Marcus and his pillars," said Julia, pushing a half-eaten honey cake aside. "You always try to be different, brother."

Marcus decided that he really didn't want to engage with a discussion of his character, so he prudently smiled and said nothing.

* * *

Eventually the dinner was consumed, the table cleared, and the diners drifted off, leaving Julia, Marcus and Lucius sipping wine. "How is Tiberius?" Marcus asked Julia.

"He is making a name for himself and our family," interjected Lucius. "He says the emperor thinks highly of him."

Julia glanced sidelong at her husband, who was slightly drunk, then arched her eyebrows at Marcus. Lucius did not notice, continuing to boast about his brother-in-law. Then he arose, announced that he was going to take a nap and wobbled off.

When he had left, Marcus asked again about their older brother.

Julia shrugged. "Tiberius is Tiberius. He always has a plan, and it generally is aimed at increasing his status. He says it is for the family, but, then again, since mother and father are gone, he thinks of himself as the family. So, nothing much has changed, dear brother."

Marcus chuckled. "We grow older but when we are together it is as if we were all children again."

Julia nodded. "And when you have children of your own that can get awkward," she said.

Marcus looked at his sister warmly. On the surface she seemed shallow, but she was intelligent and a careful observer. Growing up, she was always the quiet watcher. In those days she had said little, but she could startle you with her insight. And there was a bond between them—two outsiders leaning on one another in order to survive their warring older brothers and indifferent father.

"He maneuvers for position, brother, and he is good at it, although maybe not quite as good as he thinks he is," she said quietly, "but he did choose the winner in the battle between Philip and Decius."

Marcus nodded. "He did, and we should give him credit," he said.

"Or Fortuna," said Julia sipping her wine.

Marcus laughed. "So, do we know where things stand with our family and the emperor?"

Julia shrugged. "I do not pay a lot of attention to politics, brother, I leave that to Sabina."

"She is much like you, Julia," said Marcus. "You always listened better than any of the rest of us."

"Well, you're men," she said with a small smile. "Women have to listen."

"So, we are safe?" he asked.

"It would seem so," she replied, "although with Tiberius's maneuvers, one can never be sure. And look at you. Head of a legion, a hero, that also counts, Marcus. You have done well, brother."

"I guess," he said, "although, between us, there were times I didn't know what I was doing."

"Oh, I think you did. It is just that in our family, competence was recognized only in those above us, so we are never sure," she said with a smile. "My friends all think you are a hero, which annoys Tiberius no end."

Marcus laughed out loud. "Some things never change, sister, do they?"

"At least not in our family, brother," she said, rising to clear the wine goblets.

* * *

The atrium was filled with luggage, sacks of foodstuffs and jars of oil, preserved fruits and wine. Marcus and Flavius had arranged for carts to haul it all to the new domus, a sprawling house that faced the back of the Trajan baths and the Portico of Livia. The two men looked harassed—finding transport for six people and an enormous mound of baggage was no easy task in central Roma.

Aelia was all graceful condescension, charming Marcus's sister and brother-in-law. It took much longer than they had planned, but eventually the party got moving, the people walking, the baggage hauled behind in carts. Marcus, Flavius and Demaratus were in uniform, so navigating the crowds was less a chore as people moved aside at the sight of helmets and crests.

It was no great distance to the new domus, but the morning was warm and the press of people in the streets made it warmer still. By the time the party arrived, everyone was sweating and feeling grimy. The Roma air was thick with smoke and the odors from numerous thermopylae and fabrication workplaces that turned out everything from gold jewelry to cutlery and nails.

The staff Julia had arranged for, a man and two women, waited off to one side. Aelia pulled a large brass key from her bag and unlocked the front door, making way for the party to enter, all sighing with relief. Roma was taxing on the body.

The domus was almost twice the size of Julia and Lucius's domus, with a large atrium and spacious rooms, including a generous kitchen. There was an extensive garden, featuring a fountain with a pair of nymphs emerging from a pool. The party scattered to choose their rooms, then gathered in the garden. A trellis covered with grape vines sheltered several benches and chairs, and everyone gravitated to the welcome shade. The staff brought a tray of cups filled with wine and life began to look a little better to all.

"We must thank you for this domus, Aelia," said Flavius, the others nodding or otherwise adding their assent.

"It will do," said Aelia. Rachel and Coventina seemed to flinch a little, a reaction that Flavius put down to Aelia's breezy response. None of them could afford a house of this size and beauty, but for Aelia it was a step down from what she was used to. Clearly this made the former slave and the Celt uncomfortable, though they were careful to mask it. It didn't particularly bother the optio, but he had never been a slave or lived in a small, mountain village like that in which Coventina had grown up. Their reaction did concern him, however. He would have to talk to Demaratus and broach the subject with Rachel. Internal division was not something they could afford.

In the meantime, Flavius would happily take advantage of Aelia's affluence. He could get used to being wealthy, although the moment the thought occurred to him, he laughed to himself, "You will never be rich, Flavius Priscus. Comfortable will do just fine."

* * *

The new domus was close to the Trajan baths, and the whole party spent hours there. Since all weapons were barred, a rule strictly enforced by an army of attendants, Marcus had no worries about security. The baths included two large libraries, one Greek, one Latin, plus innumerable shops. The immense Flavian Amphitheatre was just beyond, with its enormous gilt bronze statue and the sprawling temple of Claudius. Marcus explained that the statue was originally of the emperor Nero, but it had been modified after his murder, repurposed as a devotee of sun worship. "Nero was blamed for the great fire, so no one wanted to celebrate him," explained Marcus, "but you don't just toss away a 90-foot statue."

Demaratus smiled. "Rewriting history is something every emperor does. And that trait is not confined to the Empire of Roma. You know, the statue was the work of the Greek sculptor Zenodoros," he informed them.

Marcus and Flavius glanced at each other. "So, the Greeks made all this stuff, huh?" asked Flavius.

"No," answered Demaratus, "Just the beautiful stuff."

"By the gods," murmured Flavius, deciding not to say anything else. Crossing verbal swords with the Greek was generally a losing endeavor

* * *

One afternoon the party returned from the baths to find two men loitering by the front door. Marcus started to reach for his sword, but Flavius put a restraining hand on him. "My cousins, sir. I will handle this." He turned to the party and made a round of introductions. "These are my cousins, Vibius and Numerius. You may be seeing a good deal of them while we are in Roma."

Marcus and Demaratus shook their hands and the women nodded politely, but with a certain wariness. Both men certainly had a family resemblance to Flavius. They were built much the same way—short legs, long stocky torsos, and formidable arm muscles. A red slash ran from Vibius's left ear to his cheek, and Numerius's arms were etched with scars. They did not look like the kind of people one would like to encounter at night—or during the day, for that matter.

When they were finally alone, Flavius embraced them both, and all three departed for an inn nearby. Settling around a table with a pitcher of wine, they gossiped about family for a bit. Flavius poured another round, and they got down to business. "I want to know if you lads are available," he said.

"Depends," said Vibius. "What for?"

"Bodyguards," answered Flavius.

"Who we up against?" asked Numerius.

Flavius spun his cup in his hands. "That is not clear." He told his cousins about the situation with Aelia's brother. And he told them that the Praetorian Guards might be involved.

The two men looked at one another. "Look, Flavius, we would like to help out, but we don't mess with the Guard," said Vibius.

"It wouldn't be the Praetorians themselves, but they might hire someone. My superior's family is on good terms with the new emperor, so the Guard is not going to do anything directly. But they could arrange something," said Flavius. He pulled out his purse and withdrew the gold aureus. "There is one for each of you, plus 10 denearii."

Both men looked at the gold coin and were silent for a moment. "Make it 10 denearii apiece, cousin, and we are your men," said Vibius.

"There was a time when blood ties were enough," grumbled Flavius.

"Those times are long gone, cousin," said Numerius. "If we are going up against the Guard, we need to know it is worth our while."

Flavius bit back a retort about family and loyalty. Roma was always a hard place. And it was harder today than it had been a decade ago. "Well, we need the help," he thought. "Agreed," he told them, "When can you start?"

"Day after tomorrow," answered Vibius. "We have some people to visit tomorrow."

Flavius shuddered. He wouldn't like to be one of those "people."

"One aureus now, the other when we leave. I will have half

the denarii when you show up," said Flavius. The two looked at one another and nodded.

"And keep your ears open," said Flavius. "This brother who wants to get rid of his sister may be more of a threat than the Praetorians. He's a slimy bastard, but a rich slimy bastard. He may be hiring."

"We'll keep that in mind, cousin and will ask around quietly," Vibius assured him.

Flavius poured another round, and the three fell back to family news and rumors.

XVIII

Ordinarily, Aelia would have had her lawyer come to her, but Cassius Caesennius—who had come recommended by her attorney in Corduba—said that he had someone he wanted her to meet, a senator who had known her father and who Cassius believed might lend a sympathetic ear. Aelia could not ask a senator to come to her, so she would go to him, to a domus on the Palatine Hill not far from where her party was staying. She had initially intended to walk, but Marcus insisted that she travel in a covered litter. "It is an extra layer of protection," he said. "Flavius and I will be with you in case there is any trouble."

"I thought Flavius was arranging for bodyguards," said Aelia, who was none too happy about being locked up in a curtained litter or, for that matter, having Marcus along. She wanted to keep a wall between her business and her private life, and Marcus's constant attendance made this difficult. But she was also wary of her brother.

"They will be here tomorrow. In the meantime, Flavius and I will protect you," said Marcus.

She smiled and kissed him on the cheek. "And no one could

be safer than I with two great warriors by my side. Is the litter really necessary?"

"First, no one will know who is in the litter," he answered, "and second, they would have to cast aside the curtains to attack you, and that makes them vulnerable to us."

Aelia sighed. "All right, I suppose I can't tell you your business. But I am not relying entirely on you two," she said. "I will be armed."

Normally, Marcus would have laughed at a statement like that, but not with Aelia. She had killed a man in Mauretania with a knife. Anyone who took her for a helpless woman would be in for a very uncomfortable surprise. At the same time, Aelia really had no idea what she was up against. Professional assassins were as dangerous as—or more so—than the toughest legionnaire.

A staff member knocked at the cubiculum door. "Lady Aelia, your litter is here."

Aelia gathered up a bag and pulled a wicked-looking knife from a chest near their bed. She dropped the knife and scabbard into the bag and took Marcus's arm. "Let us go forth and conquer, my noble warrior," she said with a grin.

Flavius was waiting in the atrium armed with a sword and a short-handled spear. Demaratus was with him, as were Coventina and Rachel.

"Are you sure you don't want me to come along?" asked the Greek.

"We need someone here, signifer," said Flavius. "A strike at Aelia might be indirect." He indicated the two other women.

Rachel embraced Aelia. "Be careful, sister. I want to go but was told I would be more of a hindrance than a help."

"Defending one person is easier than defending two, but I never said you would be a hindrance," Flavius said defensively.

"No, that was my word," said Rachel. She touched the optio's shoulder. "Be careful, Flavius."

Flavius reddened and coughed. Aelia raised the ghost of an eyebrow at Marcus, who hoped his awkward—and touchy—second-in-command had not noticed.

Eventually the small party got going. Four strong young slaves carried the curtained litter, and Marcus and Flavius followed slightly behind, ready to block any attempt to attack Aelia. The streets were crowded, but Flavius called out "Stand aside" in his best parade ground voice, and people moved aside, intimidated by the optio's growl and the two officers' uniforms. Nevertheless, for Marcus and Flavius it was a tense journey. It was obvious that even with the two men and the litter, Aelia was vulnerable to an attack, and two bodyguards were insufficient for the job. Both were relieved when they arrived at a large domus with an intricately carved front door.

An older woman slave answered their knock and ushered them into an atrium decorated with frescoes of animals and flowers. Cassius, the lawyer, greeted them and led them out into an extensive peristyle garden where an older man, the purple stripes on his toga announcing he was a senator, was seated under a shaded trellis. Introductions were made, and Marcus took a curule chair off to one side. The curule was made of an exotic wood that Marcus had not seen before and was furnished with a felt pillow for comfort. Flavius, recognizing that a plebeian like himself would appear out of place, quietly slipped back to the atrium.

Cassius outlined the case, while Aelia discreetly studied the senator, Gaius Julius Cornutus. The man sported several rings, one featuring a carved garnet, another a large piece of lapis. He was also adorned with a roped gold necklace and an electrum bracelet in the form of a snake. The senator was heavy, and his face was flushed. "Too much wine," thought Aelia. Indeed, Gaius was already sipping from a glass goblet, though it was not yet noon. She did not think it was water.

Aelia had dressed in a light stola and pella. She handed the latter to a young woman slave, who collected it and vanished. For jewelry, she wore only a bracelet and a simple necklace set with an emerald. The senator openly admired her, which was her intention. When the lawyer had finished, Aelia smiled.

"You knew my father," she said to the senator.

"Yes," Gaius replied. "He was most helpful in arranging a shipment of wheat from Caesarea to Roma. We met in Carthago Nova. He also visited me here on one occasion. I was fond of him, and he had a good head for business."

"He spoke well of you, Senator Julius," lied Aelia. She had, in fact, never heard her father say anything about any Roman senator. "What is your thinking on the matter of his will, Senator Julius?"

"Please, call me Gaius," he said, holding his goblet out for more wine. A slave at his elbow poured some from a silver pitcher. "Well, the matter is complex, Aelia. On one hand, the will violates a central premise of our laws. But, on the other, an emperor approved it, and directly overturning the act of an emperor is not a precedent many would like to see established. No emperor likes to think that when he passes on to godhood all his works will be dismantled."

He took a long draw from his goblet, set it down and picked up a fig from a bowl on a small table nearby. "There is also a matter of timing," he continued. "Emperor Decius is still in the process of establishing himself. Some see him as a usurper, though I am not among them. Still, Philip the Arab had supporters. Decius has appointed his oldest son, Herennius Etruscus, as his successor, but there is trouble in Dacia. The Goths threaten the border, and there is a rumor that the emperor is preparing to lead the army himself."

"How does that affect my father's will, Gaius?" asked Aelia.

"The Senate is unlikely to act without agreement from the emperor, and if the emperor is not here, well..." He trailed off mid-sentence.

"Decius must make the decision?" Aelia pressed.

"That, or make it known that he leaves the matter with the Senate," answered Gaius.

"What of the Vestal Virgins?" asked Cassius.

The senator was silent for a time. "The Virgins will not act counter to the emperor," he said, "but if Decius does not involve himself, they may act as they see fit."

"And do you know what that would be?" asked Aelia.

"The Vestal Virgins are not always predictable. But a generous donation to their temple would not go unnoticed," answered Gaius.

"That can be arranged," said Aelia. "How would they know it came from me?"

"I can make sure that they know," answered Gaius.

"I am much in your debt, Gaius," said Aelia.

The senator stirred, cleared his throat and held up his glass again. "Now I will learn what this will cost," Aelia said to herself.

"I would appreciate your help on a matter," he said. "I have invested in trade from the east. Pepper, jewels, perfumes, rare woods and such." He arose and drew her attention to a chair made of a wood that Aelia did not recognize. Its back was decorated with an ivory carving displaying exquisite workmanship—a nude dancer, full-breasted with long, braided hair, adorned with armlets and anklets, and attended by two women. It was one of the finest ivory carvings Aelia had ever seen.

"It is beautiful, Gauis," she said, running a finger over it.

"The land it comes from," said the senator, "was written about by Herodotus. According to him, gold is excavated by huge ants guarded over by griffins. Jewels are scattered like stones in the field. You have one around your neck. The riches there are beyond belief."

"I do not doubt you, Gaius," said Aelia, "but how can I be of help?"

The senator sat down again and picked up his goblet. "The riches are great, but the path to them is perilous. A ship I invested in was taken by pirates in the great sea beyond upper Aegyptus. I lost a fortune. As a senator I cannot, of course, own a ship, but I can invest in a ship's cargo. I am currently doing so, but I need other investors. The profits from my venture will return such investments four times over or more."

"I see," said Aelia. "I am interested in this, but I need to consult my financial advisor to determine what I can afford to invest. I should have such figures in a few days. Is that acceptable?"

Gaius waved his hand, "Of course. I look forward to another meeting with you."

"One more thing, senator. What would be considered a proper donation to the Virgins?" she asked.

"Hmmm," he said, looking off into the garden. "I would think 1000 sestertii would be well received."

Aelia flinched, although she hid it well. Between the Vestal Virgins and Gaius, her resources would be strained, but she estimated that she could manage it. She would have to borrow to come up with all that was required. That should not be overly difficult, although the interest was likely to be high. She didn't see that she had much choice.

It was clear the meeting was over. It ended with a round of polite patter and pledges to meet again in a few days. "I will inform Cassius when I have pulled together my resources, Senator, and we can reconvene. Is that acceptable?" asked Aelia.

"Yes, of course," said Gaius, looking anxious to leave.

Marcus had alerted Flavius and the party reassembled outside Cassius's domus. The four slaves had been waiting patiently all this time. Marcus leaned over and whispered to Aelia, "Your financial advisor?"

She smiled at him, "Demaratus."

Marcus nodded. "Right. As a sailor he will know about ships and such." He said this almost with a tremor. Talking about ships reminded him of what the sea had done to him. Aelia climbed into the litter, he and Flavius took their places, and the party headed for their new home.

XIX

The domus was in turmoil. Rachel and Coventina had cornered Flavius and insisted he act as their guide. "We want to see everything, optio," said Coventina.

"Everything?" said Flavius weakly. "Roma is a big city. They say the biggest in the world. It would take us a week to see 'everything,' and even then, we would probably miss a lot."

"Well, the important things," answered Coventina. "The Flavian Amphitheatre, the Temple of Venus, and the Temple of Jupiter."

"Also the Hall of Vesta and the Baths of Caracalla," added Rachel.

"And, of course, Trajan's Forum and the Pantheon," added Coventina. "Oh, and we want to walk so we can see everything."

"Ladies, many of these things are far apart," said Flavius. "To go from the Flavian Amphitheatre to the Mausoleum is a long distance to walk," he pleaded.

"We are strong," said Rachel, sidling up to Coventina. "Men exert themselves and then rest. Women work all the time. And if we do tire, then we will finish another day."

Flavius found that turn of the conversation alarming. He did not look forward to being a tour guide, but to do so for more than one day was unthinkable. Flavius had many virtues, but light conversation was not among them. And while he was born and raised in the city, even he had not visited every place Rachel and Coventina wanted to go.

"We are so looking forward this," said Rachel, which of course silenced any protests Flavius might have voiced.

Both women trotted off to get properly attired and to gather up the kind of things women carried when they ventured into the wider world.

* * *

Aelia and Demaratus were deep in conversation in the garden. Aelia had laid out the proposal by Senator Gaius Julius for her to invest in a shipment of goods from India. "I know you were a sailor, Demaratus. What do you think?"

Demaratus considered this carefully. "I am not an expert on trade with India, Lady Dasumi, although I know something of it. I have never been directly involved, because I have almost always served on ships that traded to the west—Hispania, Gaul, even Britannia. But I have been to Alexandria twice, and I served with sailors that plied the eastern trade."

Aelia leaned back and smiled. "Demaratus, before we go any further, we need to discuss what you call me. My name is Aelia. I suppose it could be Aelia Dasumi, but that would be awkward for all concerned."

"You are not just Aelia Dasumi," said Demaratus. "It is more complex than that."

"You mean, 'what do I call the consort of a legate?'" she said with a grin.

"Who is my superior officer," added the Greek, looking uncomfortable.

"You mean a superior officer who doesn't think he is divine and acts like an ordinary person, except when he is winning battles and outthinking his opponent?" she asked.

Demaratus smiled. "Yes, that one."

"Well, what about this? When we are with Marcus you try not to call me anything, and if you have to, say 'Lady Aelia.' When we are alone, just say Aelia."

Demaratus nodded. "An admirable compromise, Aelia," he agreed, stumbling over the name. "As to your question about the trade with India. I know that it began with my people. Strabo writes that a Greek, Eudoxus of Cyzicus, made friends with a sailor from India who had been stranded on the Erythra Thalassa—you call it Pontus Herculus—and made the trip from Aegyptus across Mare Erythraean to India. Before then, most trade had come overland. Your senator friend is correct about the potential of this trade, but I don't know exactly how much is involved or whether it is safe or not. However, I believe I can find out some of that."

Aelia shook her head. She was always amazed at how well read Demaratus was. She had heard of Strabo, but had never seen anything written by him. "Would you do that, signifer?" requested Aelia. "And while I hate to press you, I will need that information as soon as you can gather it. I know I am asking you to give up touring Roma with my sister and Coventina, and I am grateful for it."

Demaratus smiled. "You mean I am to spend the day in a cool library close to the baths rather than tramping around a hot, muggy over-crowded city to gawk at a bunch of temples? Yes, Aelia, you ask much."

Aelia laughed out loud. "You do not want to spend a day gazing on the beauty of columns and pediments?"

The Greek shrugged. "You got them from us, remember?"

"You are fun, Demaratus," said Aelia. "And if you are ever uncertain about how to address me, think of the first time we met. As I recall, I was covered in blood and we were in rather a hurry."

The signifer chuckled. "That is not image I am likely to forget, Aelia. I also remember you were holding a knife and that the blood was not your own. Why do you think I am always polite to you?"

Aelia smiled and grasped him by the hand. "Thank you, my friend."

Demaratus nodded and rose. "I hope to have something for you by tonight."

* * *

Flavius was juggling. Demaratus had just informed him that he would be unable to accompany the party of tourists because of the mission Aelia had given him, and there was no arguing with that. But Flavius had been depending on Demaratus for help squiring around Rachel and Coventina, and also for extra security. Now he would have to decide whether to take one of his cousins and leave the other with Marcus and Aelia, or leave both at the domus.

The sensible thing was to take a bodyguard, but Flavius was reluctant to have one of his cousins hanging around while the women looked at temples and tombs. Most of all, he didn't want to look stupid in front of a cousin and, given his awkwardness with women, that was a strong possibility. But this required an okay from Marcus, who correctly pointed out the problem of a single person defending two others in a crowded city.

"They aren't after me and the girls, sir, they want you and Aelia," Flavius argued.

"I wouldn't make the assumption that they are just after me and Aelia," Marcus said. "They know of you and the signifer and may strike at us through others."

"I know, sir, but her brother is the greatest danger to your lady." Flavius, too, had difficulty using her first name. "I doubt that the Guard will try something openly, what with you being a legate and all that."

"It hasn't stopped them from killing emperors," Marcus countered.

"True, but that's different. I mean I can't say exactly why, but it is," said Flavius. "You need Viblius and Numerius, sir."

"Rough looking pair, optio," said Marcus raising an eyebrow.

"And that's just what we are looking for, sir. You don't have to invite them for dinner," said Flavius somewhat defensively. Although he wasn't feeling so much defensive as harassed and apprehensive about how the day would go. He wanted to make a good impression on Rachel, and coordinating the tour as well as security was just too much.

Marcus intuited this. "I think you are right, Flavius. Just be careful."

"I will, sir," he said.

Flavius slipped out the front door and waved Viblius and Numerius over. The two had been lounging against a wall across the street.

"What's up, cousin?" asked Viblius.

Flavius outlined security for the day. "Marcus will be in the domus," he said. "The only way in is the front door. There is a side door off the kitchen, but it leads to an alley with a locked gate. Stay within view of the door, but don't look like you are bodyguards."

Numerius stared at him coldly. "We know our business, Flavius. Unless it's a bunch of Praetorians, no one is getting into that house."

Flavius nodded. "All right, but if there is an attempt on the domus, fall back to the front door. It will be unlocked. Defend the door and call for Marcus."

"Can he fight?" asked Viblius.

"He can fight," Flavius assured him.

Both men nodded at him, walked across the street and conferred with one another.

Flavius went back inside to find Rachel and Coventina in the atrium, each with a bag and dressed for a march into the heart of Roma. "Give me a moment," he said, as he went to his room. He was dressed in a uniform sans helmet. The latter would be out of place in the temples that the women wanted to visit. He belted a gladis sword on his left, slipped a pugio dagger into the belt, and covered both with a light cloak. He considered the short spear but rejected it. One does not go into temples carrying spears.

Striding back to the atrium, he said, "Ladies, let us go forth. There is a city to be sacked."

The quip drew a solid laugh from both women. So, a good start.

* * *

Demaratus headed for the Forum of Trajan, which hosted two massive libraries, one for Greek tomes, the other for Latin. He considered the Greek library, but it would include mostly history. He needed current information, and that would be housed in the Latin library. Both stood opposite the great column of Trajan, recording the emperor's conquest of Dacia. The library included a large central reading room and two floors of books and scrolls.

He knew the drill—stand gazing at the shelves and look confused and intimidated. Such an expression immediately draws a librarian.

"May I help you, sir?" asked an older man dressed in a simple but well-made tunic and pants. Demaratus was glad he was wearing his uniform. He explained what he was looking for, adding that he was particularly interested in records of import taxes.

"Ah, yes, taxes," said the librarian. "Many pray to Mercury and Fortuna to reveal the secrets of wealth, but a good tax roll will do that without a donation at their temples. We have such records, although I think I might introduce you to a shortcut."

"That would be most kind of you," said Demaratus, hesitating, so as to encourage the librarian to give his name.

"Lucius Attius, sir. It is always an honor to help those who serve. Follow me." He turned and led Demaratus out of the reading room into a side anteroom containing several long tables. People were reading scrolls and books by oil lamps, although enough light spilled through the enormous windows to make the lamps almost superfluous.

Lucius stopped at a table at which sat one of the oddest-looking people Demaratus had ever encountered. The man was hunched over, holding a glass bound to a short handle. The signifer had seen one of these before, though they were fairly rare. Held close to the eye and the scroll, the glass magnified images.

The man was completely bald, although he was hardly old. Indeed, he looked to be in his late twenties. Besides having no hair on his head, he also had no eyebrows, although two were drawn with what looked to be pencil. He wore a shapeless garment that Demaratus could not place. The man looked up at the librarian, squinting with nearsightedness. "Yes?" he asked in a voice that was almost a whisper.

"Sextus Cornelius. I have here a soldier of the Empire who needs to know about trade and taxes," said Lucius. "Is there anyone in Roma who knows more than you?"

"No," replied the man and went back to squinting at his scroll.

The librarian glanced at Demaratus, arched an eyebrow and mouthed "patience."

Demaratus nodded he understood.

"He has some questions, sir. Could you find the time to answer them?" asked Lucius.

There was a long silence. Finally, the man said, "Why?" without looking up.

"I am an officer of the VII Legion Hispania," replied Demaratus. "As the chief financial officer"—a major exaggeration—"of the VII Legion, it is important for me to understand the fiscal basis for supporting my unit of the Roman Army. The army," he said sweeping his arm around the library, "that makes all of this possible."

Sextus looked up. "Hispania is not very important," he said and went back to his scroll.

The librarian started to protest, but Demaratus waved him to silence. Pressing this odd man was not liable to be useful. But provoking a mild disagreement might yield something. "Hispania and Mauretania provide more wheat to Roma than Aegyptus. Silver from our southern mountains underlies our coinage. Italia relies on our fish sauce, garam. Gold from our northern mountains and tin from Britannia, and much of the wealth of Gaul, flows through our ports. You call that 'unimportant'?"

The man sighed. "One of your legionnaires earns around 700 to 800 sesterces per annum. Last year a single shipment of 150 tons of ivory, perfume, tortoise shell and textiles from the east was valued at nine million sesterces, That would purchase a major estate in Italia or nine seats in the Senate. The import tax paid on that shipment was over two million sesterces. Imports from India through Aegyptus are worth over one billion sesterces per year, of which the empire takes 270 million sesterces. Your legion? The cost of supporting eight legions to defend our northern borders is 88 million sesterces per year. One third of our Empire's tax revenues come directly from our trade with India." The man finally looked up and squinted. "So, sir, you and your province are not very important. Now if you will forgive me, I have work." And with that he went back to his reading.

The librarian looked shocked, but Demaratus tapped his arm

to say everything was fine. "I thank you, Sextus Cornelius," he said. The man did not look up or acknowledge him.

The librarian apologized to Demaratus as they left the room and re-entered the main reading room. "He is an odd person, sir," said Lucius, "and rude beyond measure."

The signifer laughed. "Experts are many times that way. The army has to deal with engineers who talk to us as if we were dim-witted children, and he seems to know what he is talking about."

"Oh, I can vouch for that," said Lucius. "He is considered the most knowledgeable person in Roma on the subject of taxes."

"My major interest was in the value of the eastern trade, and he gave me that. I have what I need," said Demaratus. "Or almost."

"What else do you require?" asked Lucius.

"People who can talk to me about the trade itself, sailors and ship captains," replied Demaratus.

"I would think the docks, sir. Or if you have the time, Ostia," said Lucius.

"I don't, so I will hope there is someone knowledgeable near the river."

"Good luck, sir," said Lucius.

"And thanks to you, Lucius. This has been most helpful," said Demaratus.

* * *

After five hours of temples, markets, basilicas, and forums, Flavius was exhausted. Coventina and Rachel had dragged him back to the Imperial Forum so that they could shop for jewelry.

The optio was leaning up against a wall, silently praying for a place to sit. His plan had been to walk the two women into the ground in a few hours, and then swing back to the Trajan Baths, but as he had discovered numerous times in war, no plan survives contact with the enemy.

He had started with the Flavian amphitheater and the plaza to its front, featuring the elegant Temple of Venus and the huge bronze-gilt statue of the sun god. The Imperial Forum was next, with its porticos and shops and enormous temple to Mars Ultor. The temple was impressive, featured Mars leaning on his spear, with Venus and Fortuna on either side, and the actual sword of Caesar. Flavius explained that the temple was also associated with Romulus and the Goddess Roma. "This is very much a temple of the city," he said, pointing out a statue of Aeneas. "He came from Troy and founded Roma."

Coventina and Rachel looked a bit lost. "What is Troy?" the Celt asked, drawing Flavius into a long explanation of the Trojan wars that eventually had both women looking bored.

"Let's go see the Temple of Vesta," said Rachel. "I want to see the virgins. Is it true that some of them were buried alive?"

Flavius explained that it was unlikely they would see any of the six virgins, because they generally remained ensconced in the Vestal House, but that the temple was open to the public. And, yes, if a virgin violated the rules, she was lowered into a cistern with a loaf of bread and a single lamp and then sealed in. "They serve for thirty years," he said, "and they are greatly respected."

"Why?" asked Rachel.

"They represent the family and the empire, and they guard the sacred flame. The temple also contains the Palladium, the wooden image of Athena that Aeneas brought all the way from Troy," Flavius explained. And indeed, the temple was impressive, although the Palladium itself was not. "It's just a wooden statue," sniffed Coventina.

"It is hundreds of years old, and it's said to have been taken by Ulysses himself," protested Flavius, beginning to feel defensive.

"Who is Ulysses?" asked Coventina. That sparked another lecture, this one on the sack of Troy and the Odyssey, which only led to more glazed eyes.

Flavius herded them out of the temple and put the party on a street leading to the Palatine Hill topped by the massive Temple of Jupiter and the sprawling Emperor's Palace, with its public gardens and fountains, exactly what the optio needed. As they emerged from the Temple of Vesta, they encountered a procession of musicians and carts filled with bread, led by a russet-colored dog.

"What is that?" asked Coventina.

"It celebrates Robigus," answered Flavius. "Uh, Robigus is the god of wheat rust and mildew."

"Mildew has a god?" asked a dubious Rachel.

"Wheat rust and mildew can be a problem," explained Flavius.

"But doesn't the goddess Ceres take care of that?" asked Coventina. "We celebrate Ceres in Hispania, even among my people."

"Well, it's complicated, and I don't understand all of it myself. I am not a farmer or a baker, but they seem to think it's important, and that's what matters, right? said Flavius.

"What does that have to do with a dog?" both women asked at the same time, then looked at one another and giggled.

"Uh, well, they sacrifice a red dog, because, uh, it is the color of wheat rust."

"They kill a dog to keep mildew away?" Coventina shook her head. "Romans are so odd."

"Now look, Coventina, I don't make fun of your religion," said Flavius, becoming increasingly annoyed.

"But that's because you consider us barbarians," she reminded him. "We all have to worship divine Augustus. We don't ask you to pay homage to our gods."

Flavius was about to say that the Romans didn't worship Celtic gods because the Romans had conquered Coventina's people, and that's what happens when you get defeated, but he quickly realized that a statement like that would be disastrous, so he simply shrugged ill-temperedly.

Flavius's favorite of the sites they visited was the Temple of Saturn Concord, with its gilded bronze measurements of the distance between each of the Empire's provincial cities to Roma. "All roads lead to Roma," said Flavius.

Coventina shrugged. "Roma depends on those cities to feed and clothe its inhabitants. Roads run in both directions."

That remark irritated Flavius, but he again decided to say nothing. He hesitated to annoy the Celt. He was hoping she would be helpful in his courtship of Rachel.

The massive Circus Maximus impressed the women. "It can sit 300,000 citizens," Flavius told them. From there they went to the Basilica Aemila, decorated with bronze battering rams captured from the battle of Aetius. "That was the battle that made Augustus emperor, ending the realm of Anthony and Cleopatra, the pharaoh of Aegyptus," Flavius lectured.

Rachel knew the story, but Coventina did not. So that required yet another history lesson. Coventina's only comment was, "Sad." Flavius had no idea what she meant, but he did not want to set off an argument. He was tiring of biting his tongue.

They marched on to the Campus Martius. The Pantheon, with its columns of polished Aegyptus marble, greatly impressed both women, which put Flavius in a better mood. But when the party finally swung back toward the Imperial Forum, Flavius's spirits flagged. He hated shopping.

Coventina was examining some gold earrings, and Rachel was trying on necklaces and admiring them in a mirror.

"Flavius, would you help, please?" Rachel asked. He was feeling grumpy enough that he considered refusing, but pushed himself away from the wall and slouched over to the jewelry store. "Would you fasten this?" she asked Flavius, who reached for the clasp.

"Flavius," she whispered. "Look into the mirror. Do you see that man with the bag around his shoulder?"

Flavius noticed that Rachel had angled the mirror not to look at herself but at the people crowding the shops and markets. It took him a moment, but he finally located the man Rachel referred to.

"Don't look directly at him," she whispered. "He has been following us since this morning. I first spotted him in the forum, and he has kept us company ever since."

Flavius mastered the urge to turn and look. "Are you sure?" he asked.

"Certain," she answered. "Now latch the clasp and act like we are talking about buying something."

"I should go grab him," said Flavius.

"No!" protested Rachel, her voice still a whisper. "He thinks we don't know he is watching us. Let him think we are oblivious. If you seize him that will alert whoever hired him. Knowledge is power, optio. We know that man is following us, but that man does not know we know that. If we seize him, they will be more careful next time.

"Ever since the forum this morning? How were you alerted to him?" asked Flavius, puzzled.

Rachel picked through a display of rings before replying. "Slaves notice things that those who have not been enslaved do not. We have no choice. We pay close attention to everything around us because if we get something wrong, we are beaten. Or worse. It is second nature to us."

"But you are not a slave," said Flavius.

She faced him with a level stare. "I am not a slave now, Flavius, but I had been a slave since I was born. I do not quickly cast aside the training of a lifetime. Slaves must always be aware of the gaze of others. Most people pass us by with but a glance, but this man kept his eyes on us the whole time we were in the forum. He is good at disguising it, but he is no match for a slave."

"Then we are in danger," said Flavius, mastering an impulse to put his hand on his gladis.

"I think not," said Rachel. "We are being tracked, but I doubt that any attempt will be made on us in such public places. But I think it prudent for us to go directly to the domus and bypass the baths of Diocletian."

Flavius nodded. "I'll go get Coventina," he said. "Stay here."

Within minutes Flavius returned with an annoyed Coventina,

whom Rachel pulled aside to whisper what was afoot. When Coventina immediately touched her thigh, Flavius realized she was armed.

The three gathered up their purchases and departed the forum, although Flavius did not relax until they were in sight of the domus and his cousins.

Once inside, Flavius went off to brief Marcus, and Coventina and Rachel took their purchases to the garden. When they were alone, Rachel turned to Coventina and asked, "Do your people have slaves?"

The Celt nodded. "We do, but it is different with us."

"Different how?" asked Rachel, putting aside her purchases.

Coventina thought for a while about how best to explain it. "Most of our slaves are captives of war. We rarely buy them as the Romans do. And while they do things like fetch, cook, help in the fields and take care of animals, there are not a lot of them. With the Romans, slaves do everything. They grow and harvest the crops, they mine gold and silver, they make fish sauce, and they build roads and houses. Sometimes I am not sure the Romans do anything but tell slaves what to do."

Rachel smiled. "It does seem that way. We also raise their children and make their clothes. Tell me, do your people beat them?"

Coventina looked uncomfortable. "Some masters beat their slaves, but if they do, the slaves run away. And there is no army or vigiles like the Romans have to hunt them down or keep them in line. So, it is generally thought to be a bad idea," she said. "Were you beaten?"

Rachel nodded. "On occasion, but I was a household slave

who raised my master's children. We were privileged, or at least more so than the slaves in the mines and the fields."

Coventina shook her head. "I don't think of slaves much," she said. "I never had one. We were a poor family."

Rachel was silent, looking off into the garden. "I think I made Flavius uncomfortable today when I told him slaves see things that others don't."

"I think you make Flavius uncomfortable for a lot of reasons that don't have anything to do with slavery," suggested Coventina.

Rachel smiled and arched an eyebrow.

"You must know that he is taken with you, Rachel," continued Coventina.

"Yes, I do," she said quietly.

"Do you feel the same?" pressed Coventina.

"I like him a lot. He is more interesting than he initially seems. He is also intelligent and kind, though he can be very awkward," she replied.

Coventina laughed. "Most men are, and the ones who are not are generally not to be trusted. My Greek being the exception."

Rachel smiled. "He is smooth, isn't he?"

"You have no idea," said Coventina. "But I have found that awkward is not always a bad trait."

"No, I agree," said Rachel. "In Flavius, it is sort of sweet. He is this great warrior who trips over his tongue in my presence."

"Are you worried that he thinks of you as a slave?" asked Coventina.

"No. One of the things that makes him attractive to me is

that he obviously sees me as a woman. Slaves never make anyone feel awkward," Rachel observed.

"Will you encourage him? asked Coventina.

Rachel was silent for a time. "We will see," she said. "I need a bath," she added, clearly putting an end to subject.

XX

Julius Dasumi and Gnaeus Domitius faced each other across the small table. A note the previous day had instructed Julius to wear the same cloak and return to the same spot at the Baths of Diocletian. Gnaeus was late but gave no explanation. Once again, Julius trailed him through the Roman crowds to the deserted shop.

The two sat silently, each waiting for the other to begin. "What do you plan?" Julius finally asked the man.

"First things, first," replied Gnaeus. "There are complications."

"And by 'complications,' you mean I have to pay you more, am I right?" asked Julius, not trying to keep the sarcasm from his voice.

The man shrugged. "Do it yourself and save the money."

"I can't take on three soldiers, and you know it," flared Julius.

"Well, that's one of the complications," said Gnaeus.

"What do you mean?" asked Julius.

"You didn't to tell me who these soldiers were," replied Gnaeus. "Your sister's boyfriend is the legate of a legion, a legion that just successfully liberated a city in Hispania. The Empire doesn't get a lot of victories these days, so these 'three soldiers' sort of stand out. You also didn't tell me that they have a couple of bodyguards."

Julius shifted in his chair. "I didn't know anything about bodyguards, but can't you just take them out? As for Marcus and his officers, he is an acting legate, and he may or may not get his appointment approved. He doesn't have a lot of influence in Hispania."

"He may not amount to much where you come from," countered Gnaeus, "but his family is well thought of by the new emperor. They backed Decius against Philip, and we know who came out on top of that one."

Julius shrugged. "So, it is going to cost me more. How much?"

Gnaeus smiled. "Fifty aurei."

"What? You can't be serious," Julius said. "That's a small fortune!"

"A pittance compared to what you gain if we succeed, Dasumi. That's the price. Take it or leave it," said Gnaeus quietly.

Julius fumed, mumbling to himself. After some time, he said, "All right. When do you need it?"

"Half of it before we act, the other half when the job is done," Gnaeus answered.

"I will have 25 aurei tomorrow. Where do I take the money?" asked Julius.

"Same place tomorrow, same time," answered Gnaeus.

Julius rose and left without a word. Gnaeus watched him go and frowned. "This could be trouble," he thought. Killing someone was one thing, taking on three soldiers was another. He had taken the job for a reason that he knew and Dasumi did not.

He had gleaned that the Praetorian Guard also had a grievance against this legate, so the investigation that would follow an assassination might not be all that thorough. Indeed, he might be doing the Guard a favor. And 50 aurei would make him a wealthy man. Every opportunity had its risks.

Gnaeus considered his plan. He had had the optio and two of the women followed, so he had some idea of what they were like. The optio was clearly dangerous and would require at least two men to deal with him. The Greek had been followed as well, and Gnaeus was still trying to puzzle out what the man was up to. He had spent time in the library at the Trajan Forum, and then the rest of the day talking with sailors and ship captains down by the docks. The Greek was slight, so one big man should be able to deal with him. Then there was the legate, whom he assumed was past his fighting prime, and the two bodyguards. He would assign two men to the legate, one to each of the body-guards, and two others assigned to kill the Dasumi woman. Nine men ought to be able to do the job, but they would have to be good. Speed was essential. Get in, kill, then vanish. He wouldn't have to kill the three soldiers or the bodyguards, just keep them busy. If the two other women got in the way, well, that would be their funeral. But women screamed and cried, they didn't fight. It could be done.

But there was an easier way to do it, one that would save a lot of money. Poison was cheap. Gnaeus knew a man who could brew up a deadly potion that would do the job without the drama of an assassination in a public place. The poison could be delivered by an insider. A member of the serving staff the Dasumi woman had hired was the sister of one of his enforcers.

She could be pressured to serve poisoned wine. If it worked, he would be a rich man for the price of a good quality toga. If it failed, well, he could always fall back to the original plan.

XXI

Tribune Antonius Clodius sat quietly in the outer office of Praetorian Guard Legate Aeilus Hadrianus Marullinos, rolling and unrolling a small scroll. Finally, a clerk—whose name quite escaped him—called him in. "The legate will see you now, Tribune," he said, saluting him. Antonius gave him a perfunctory salute and strode into the office, closing the door behind him.

"Sir," he said, saluting the man seated at a small desk. The office was sparsely furnished and without adornment. There were two additional chairs, a long chest with several drawers and a small cabinet. Aelius Hadrianus was a grave and watchful man, lean and mostly bald. His only jewelry was a gold bracelet and a signet ring. He had mastered the art of remaining expressionless, although his eyes were piercing. "Tribune," he said quietly, pushing some papers to one side.

"Sir," Antonius said again. "I want to report to you about Marcus Favonius."

"Begin," said the legate quietly. The clerk had been banished. Roma has a thousand ears and what they were going to talk about was not something he wanted to be shared widely.

"We have kept an eye on the centurion and his companions, Legate, but the matter is growing quite complex," replied Antonius.

"How so?" asked Aelius, going to the chest and pulling out a small pitcher and two cups. Pouring out two servings, he handed one to the tribune and set the other on the desk, sat down and took a drink.

Antonius thanked him and took a sip himself. "Favonius and his party are being followed," he said.

The legate frowned. "Didn't you just tell me you were keeping an eye on them?"

"Yes, but our man spotted another who followed Marcus's optio, Flavius Priscus, as he showed off Roma to two women in the party, a Celt and a former slave who aided Aelia Dasumi when she was a captive of the Mauri in Mauretania last year," said the tribune.

"Who else is involved with this?" asked Antonius.

"The man who followed the party works for a man named Gnaeus Domitius," replied Antonius. "He is the head of a gang that offers protection to merchants, loans out money at exorbitant interest rates, and can be hired for anything from theft to murder."

"And why is this man not shoveling salt or hauling marble somewhere," asked the legate, sitting back and folding his arms.

The tribune shrugged. "People find him useful, and he is careful about whose toes he steps on. He also lends money to senators at much lower interest rates."

The legate smiled. "So, a useful thug who does the dirty work for those who want to keep their hands clean."

"Exactly," said Antonius. "As I said, he has uses."

"Who is using him?"

"That would be Aelia Dasumi's brother," answered the tribune.

"Do you know for what purpose?" asked Aelius.

"We are not certain, but I assume it is to eliminate her. The brother, Julius Dasumi, has engaged several senators in his efforts to break his father's will and assume control of the family's wealth. As written, the will evenly divides the estate between the brother and the sister."

The legate frowned. "I recall that from our last discussion on this matter. How is that possible?"

"The father was close to Emperor Gordian III, who pressured the Senate to set aside our laws of inheritance and grant an equal division of the property. It is quite a fortune. The brother is pouring gold and silver into hands all over Roma."

The legate smiled. "A wealthy provincial who thinks that gold can buy anything, is he?"

"Yes," answered Antonius, "and in truth, it is generally true. But as I said, this matter is complex,"

"Remind me," said Aelius, taking another sip of wine. "And sit."

"Thank you, sir," said the tribune, who sat and ran his hands through his hair, gathering his thoughts. "The family of Marcus has chosen wisely in the dispute between Philip and Decius. The emperor has been rewarding such loyalty with gifts and appointments, and one of Marcus's brothers is lobbying to be appointed a senator, although I think he would accept a lesser post. He is ambitious. It was Marcus's other brother," he said, glancing at his scroll, "a Mamercus Favonius, who killed one of our men and wounded another while resisting an arrest ordered by Emperor Philip. His death was considered an act of loyalty to Decius."

"With the death of one of our men," said the Legate quietly.

The tribune nodded. "Add to that the suspicion that Marcus Favonius was involved in the deaths of two Praetorians in Hispania, and there is much that family has to answer for."

Aelius rose and began pacing, saying nothing for several minutes. The tribune had learned to be patient when his commander was thinking, so he stayed seated and sipped his wine.

"We must proceed with caution," the legate said, continuing to pace. "The Guard was careful to remain neutral between Philip and Decius, and that was a wise move. We must not do anything that might endanger our current relationship to the emperor. An open fight with the Favonius family is not in our interests."

"But, sir, we have lost three men to this family," protested the tribune. "Can we let that pass?"

Aelius grimaced. "Two of those men were about to be sent to the marble quarries, and we should not have gotten involved in trying to arrest Mamercus Favonius. Some of those near to Decius raised this with the emperor. I had to explain that we had no choice. It was a direct order from Philip. I pointed out that no emperor would be happy with a Praetorian Guard that did not follow orders. The issue blew over, but we must be careful that it is not revived."

The legate continued pacing. "And we need to be careful with this Marcus and his men. They defeated the Franks and lifted the siege of Tarraco, which is more than our northern legions have done in a long time. When we sent our men against him, he was a centurion on the run. Now he is acting legate of a legion that is being hailed as saviors in Hispania."

"So, we do nothing?" said Antonius incredulously.

"We watch and listen, tribune. If this Julius Dasumi kills his sister and her party, including Marcus and his officers, that is no concern of ours. Let the Vigiles handle it," he said, adding, "but an opportunity for revenge might present itself at some point, so keep up the surveillance."

"Yes, sir," answered Antonius.

"This Marcus Favonius is an interesting man, tribune," said Aelius. "From what I have heard he was outnumbered by the Franks, but he pulled off a ruse by dressing auxiliaries up as the VII Legion."

"I had not heard this, sir. Why did he do that?" asked the tribune.

Aelius chuckled. "While the Franks were concentrating on what they thought was the VII Legion, he used a flank march to approach them from the rear and cut them off from Tarraco. The entire Frankish army surrendered."

"A dangerous man," said the tribune.

"Well, at least a clever one," said the legate. "And right now in good odor with the emperor. We need to be careful." "There is another matter I would like you to look into," he added.

"Sir?" said Antonius.

"It is a matter more delicate than this business with the Favonius family," said Aelius. "Find out what you can about why the Gaul legions allowed the Frankish army to pass the length of the province unmolested."

The tribune frowned. "Why is that of interest to us, sir?"

"Some of the provinces are drifting away from Roma, and there are rumors of independent empires being established in the north and the east. Such moves toward independence weaken the Empire. That is of concern to us."

"Yes, sir," said Antonius, standing and saluting. "I will keep you informed, legate."

Aelius nodded and returned to the papers on his desk. The tribune knew when he was being dismissed.

XXII

Demaratus and Aelia were deep in conversation in the atrium when Flavius, Rachel and Coventina arrived back at the domus. The distance between the Forum and the house was short, but Flavius was tense. It took enormous discipline not to keep glancing over his shoulder to see if their shadow was still tracking them, but he recognized the wisdom of Rachel's argument—don't let the enemy know you are onto them. But who was the "enemy"? Aelia's brother or the Praetorians? He wanted to get Marcus and Demaratus together and talk about it at once, but that would have to wait. Waiting did nothing to relieve his tension. The women had gone off to the garden and were deep in conversation, so there was nothing to do but pour himself a cup of wine and sit in the kitchen. The optio was not known for his patience, but wait he did.

* * *

"This is good news," said Aelia. "I knew that the eastern trade was lucrative, just not as lucrative as you have discovered. This seems an intelligent investment."

"I agree," said Demaratus, "although it does have its risks."

"Everything has risks, signifer,' said Aelia. "A summer storm might sink a grain shipment, but investing in grain has added much to my wealth."

Demaratus nodded. "I have to say, however, that the information on the maritime aspect of this trade is mostly secondhand. I talked with several captains and sailors, but only two of the latter have actually been to a port on the Erythara Thalassa, and none have made the journey to India. While Greeks initially made that voyage, it is now dominated by the Indians themselves."

"How does that create problems?" Aelia asked.

"On the contrary. Given the presence of pirates, it may do the opposite. From what the sailors told me, the Indian ships are very large and well defended," he told her. "Of course, the profits are also lower. Large ships and defenders have to be paid for, and there are middlemen who skim off goods moving to the Mare Internum."

Aelia shrugged. "There are middlemen everywhere, Demaratus. It is the cost of doing business. The point is that such an investment is not simply throwing money away on a bribe. It is a bribe with benefits."

Demaratus laughed. "I like that."

Aelia sat back and thought for a while. "I need to gather some resources, Demaratus. I have a great deal with me, but I need to visit a bank, the one my family has dealt with for many years. I will send them a note in the morning."

"Is there anything more I can do?" asked Demaratus.

"No, you have done a great deal already. You should talk to Flavius. He looked like he wanted to interrupt our conversation but then thought better of it. In any case, he did not look very happy," Aelia said.

Demaratus had only vaguely noted that Rachel and Coventina had returned, and he hadn't paid any attention to Flavius. Aelia's ability to do several tasks at once always amazed him. "I shall do so, Aelia," he said and went looking for Flavius.

* * *

Flavius looked both tired and tense, and Demaratus had learned that a tense superior officer could sometimes make life difficult for those beneath him. He first thought to tease the optio about letting the women run him into the ground, but he restrained himself. Instead, he took a serious tone. "How did it go, comrade?"

"We were followed, signifer. Rachel spotted him this morning and kept an eye on him the whole day. Didn't say a word to me until just before we got home," he replied. He shook his head. "I don't know how I missed him."

"Spotting a single person in a city like Roma is more a matter of luck than skill," reassured Demaratus, hoping to soothe his friend.

"Relying on luck gets you killed, signifer. I didn't do my job," protested Flavius.

Attempting to turn Flavius's mind away from self-reproach, Demaratus asked, "Do you have any idea who he is?"

"No. Rachel says she spotted him because she used to be a slave, and slaves pay closer attention to the world around them than non-slaves," he replied.

Demaratus considered this. "I imagine that is true," he said thoughtfully. "Smart woman. We need to report this to Marcus."

"You think I wasn't going to?" snapped Flavius.

Demaratus bit his tongue—never argue with a superior officer in the Roman Army—then said, "I think he is reading in the library," although calling the small room with its very limited selection of books and scrolls a "library" was a stretch.

"Go get him," said Flavius.

Demaratus resented Flavius taking out his angry self-criticism at not spotting the tracker on an underling, but that was the way of the army. So the signifer went to fetch Marcus who was, indeed, in the library, but he was reading something he had brought from Hispania rather than the limited reading matter therein. He looked up when Demaratus entered, and the signifer quickly filled him in on what Flavius had said.

"Where is Flavius?" asked Marcus. Informed he was in the kitchen, he motioned for Demaratus to lead the way and followed the signifer.

When they were all together, Flavius repeated what he had told Demaratus, with a few more details about the man tracking them and how Rachel had used a mirror to show Flavius the man without revealing that they knew what he was about.

"Clever woman," noted Marcus.

"She is that," said Flavius, "but it was my job, not hers, to spot something like that."

Marcus smiled. "With the crowds in the streets, I am not certain you could spot anything smaller than an elephant trailing you. The question is who is following us and what do we do about it?"

"Somehow I don't think he was from the Praetorian Guard," said Demaratus.

"Why?" asked Flavius.

"I imagine they are much more sophisticated," he replied. As soon as it left his lips, he grew concerned that his use of 'sophisticated' might land him in trouble.

And it did.

"What are you saying, signifer, that I should have spotted our tracker because he is not as 'sophisticated' as someone from the Guard?" flared Flavius.

"That is not what I meant. It is just that I think no one—not even a clever woman like Rachel—would spot a spy from the Praetorians. And, who knows, maybe there were two spies out there" said Demaratus carefully keeping his tone neutral.

"Comrades," said Marcus breaking into the argument, "it is idle speculation to try and discover who is behind it. It happened, and the point is what do we do about it?"

Demaratus decided that it would be best if he said nothing. Anything he did say was liable to annoy the prickly optio.

Flavius shook his head. "I was the only thing between an assassin's knife and the two women," he said. "That's not good."

Demaratus thought that Flavius was not quite correct. He had seen Coventina in action, and Aelia had told of how Rachel had fought the slavers in Mauretania. Any assassin who tried to take them on might be in for a very unpleasant surprise. But he knew that saying that out loud would make everything worse.

"We were careless, I agree," said Marcus, "but that is not on you, optio. I knew you were going out in the city with Coventina and Rachel, with only yourself as security, and I saw nothing amiss. As your commander that decision rests with me."

It was a very clever way of getting Flavius to back away from his self-pity, so they could turn their attention to practical matters. Neither man could contradict a superior officer—certainly not a legate—so that was the end of it.

"What do you suggest, optio?" asked Marcus.

Flavius sighed and wiped his face. He had not bathed and felt hot and sweaty from the excursion. "Well, I think we need to stick together and never have fewer than three or four bodyguards, counting ourselves. Just going off into the city is not an option anymore."

"There could be problems with that, optio," said Marcus. "Aelia is somewhat..." He paused, reaching for a word, then continued, "private about her affairs. It took considerable pressure to have her agree that Flavius and I should accompany her to her meeting with the senator."

"And to be frank, sir, if they had come at her with half a dozen assassins, could we have stopped them?" asked Flavius.

"With you two, half a dozen wouldn't stand a chance," said Demaratus, deciding that a compliment might improve Flavius's mood.

It did.

"I honor your confidence," said Flavius in an easier tone. "But if they are watching us, they could call up more knives than even we can handle."

"Good point," said Demaratus. "Do we need more security?"

Marcus shook his head. "Where does it stop? Do we need a century? A cohort? A whole legion? I think the solution is to make sure we stay in public places and go out only when there is a maximum number of citizens in the streets."

Flavius shook his head. "I have to disagree, sir. Crowds make it hard to identify people. That's how I missed this spy. Rachel saw him because she is attuned to pay close attention to the people around her. A group of assassins can blend into a large crowd until the moment they strike. I think we should only venture out early in the morning."

"Smart," nodded Demaratus. "I propose we convey this conversation to the women, and that we make sure that we always have Rachel around when we go out in the city," a suggestion that he knew would please Flavius.

"Excellent idea, signifer," said Flavius.

Marcus suppressed a smile. "The man is good," he thought. Getting Flavius out of a bad mood is no task for an amateur.

XXIII

The conversation about security with Coventina, Rachel and Aelia over dinner the night before went well, although Aelia had looked unhappy. What she saw as a private matter had become a collective undertaking. And when all assembled the next morning to accompany Aelia to her meeting with the senator and her lawyer, problems surfaced.

Aelia refused to consider a litter. "If they are watching us, they will know who will be in the litter," she said. "I do not want to feel trapped. I will walk and that is the end of it."

Security then required creating a bubble around Aelia, with Coventina and Rachel on either side of her. Marcus took the lead, this time sporting a bronze breast plate that not only marked him as a legate—with automatic right of way—but added a layer of protection. Flavius and Demaratus manned the rear, the former in uniform, the latter in civilian garb, with Flavius's cousins on either flank. "I'm not sure this is going to work," muttered Numerius, but he and Vilaus dutifully took their places.

Assembled outside the domus, the deployment looked impressive. But as they marched through the crowded city streets, they were considerably less daunting. Marcus's uniform gave him right of way, but the residents of Roma were not easily impressed, and many did not hesitate to push back.

"Who do you think you are?"

"The legate of the Legion Hispania."

"By the Gods, provincials. Well, this is Roma, and our business is as important as yours."

It was a good thing the meeting was not far. By the time the group arrived, the "bubble" around the women had shrunk dramatically, and the VII Legion was quite humbled.

An older slave woman answered the door and escorted the party into the garden, where all were introduced to Aelia's lawyer, Cassius, and Senator Gaius Julius. Then everyone but Marcus and Aelia retired to the atrium. Marcus sat off to one side. He was an observer to this business, not a participant. The slave reappeared with wine, cups, and bowls of nuts and dates.

Aelia lifted two sacks from her bag and placed them on the small table. "Senator," she said, indicating the small bag, "I hope that Vesta smiles on our request." Reaching for the second, larger sack, she leaned forward and handed it directly to Gaius. "I am delighted to have this opportunity to invest in your endeavor, Senator," she said, "My financial advisor has convinced me that this should prove a lucrative undertaking. I see this as only the beginning of a long and fruitful partnership."

The Senator smiled broadly and gave a little bow, or as much of a bow as one can manage sitting down. "I look forward to that as well, Lady Dasumi. And I will make certain that the Vestal Virgins know of your generous donation."

"Excellent, and now I hope you can give me some idea of

the progress my brother has made with your fellow senators," she said.

Gaius sat back and picked up a goblet of wine. "It is most interesting, Lady Dasumi," he said. "He is in conversation with three of my colleagues, whom I will not name. My informants tell me that they have accepted a large sum of money from your brother, but that they are being careful. Everyone is being careful these days."

Aelia smiled, "Yes, I can imagine, but give me more details, and please call me 'Aelia'."

Gaius spread his hands. "I cannot speak to the details of any agreement between your brothers and the other senators, but I do know they are considering a petition to the Senate asking for the will to be made consistent with the law of primogeniture."

"Considering?" queried Aelia.

"As I said, everyone is being careful. No one will present a petition to the Senate unless he thinks it has the approval of the emperor, and Decius is busy planning a return to the Danubian border to confront the Goths. His son, Herennius, is to accompany him, which makes him equally as unavailable to respond to a matter like this. The youngest son, Honstilian, has only begun to occupy himself with the Senate, so I do not see him taking any kind of decisive action on your issue at this time."

"We are not unfamiliar with Emperor Decius, senator. He was, as you know, governor of my home province, Hispania, and my father knew him well," said Aelia.

"Yes, Aelia, I know this, but it appears your brother has sent a note to the emperor reminding him of his family connection and raising the issue of the will directly," noted Gaius. "I do not know how, or if, the emperor responded."

"Will the senators my brother has bribed,"—at this last word Gaius flinched— "bring up the will if the emperor does nothing? Given that Decius is planning a war, failing to respond to my brother's letter would not be at all unusual," pressed Aelia.

"Possibly. If they think the emperor is neutral, they will do so, of that I am certain," said Gaius.

"What would be the outcome in that case?" asked Aelia.

"The will would be overturned," the Senator replied.

"That would be a shame, Gaius. If I lose my portion of the will, I will have nothing more to invest in your trade endeavor, and we would both be the poorer for it," Aelia reminded him.

"I am aware of that, Aelia. In that case, I have a plan," said Gaius.

Aelia arched an eyebrow. "And that is?"

"The Senate is a body that lives by rules. There are rules for talking, rules for arguments, rules for voting. I am well versed in these areas, and I think I can use them to our mutual advantage," he explained. "But it's best not to go into details," he added, "Roma has ears."

"I defer to your experience," said Aelia.

Gaius rose from the couch. "I have much to do. I have made arrangements to meet with the Pontifex Maximus of the Vestal Virgins."

All of them stood up, and the senator left.

"Who is the Pontifex Maximus, and what are our chances?" asked Aelia, turning to Cassius.

"He is the head priest of the city and oversees the Virgins," the lawyer replied. "And I think our chances are better than they were yesterday. Gaius is a clever man and he has allies among the senators. And it is also true that he is a master of the Senate's arcane rules. But most of all, it is in his interests for you to keep your portion of the estate. In the end, that will be what's most important."

"The Vestal Virgins?" asked Aelia.

Cassius paused. "That is something I have little experience with, Aelia. But I am sure Gaius will let them know who is behind the donation. Will that influence them? I don't know. The Virgins are a bit of a mystery," he said, adding "but it won't hurt."

"The pain will be to my income, Cassius," said Aelia, waving off what looked to be the beginning of a protest. "I know, I know, you have to spend money to make money. I am well versed in matters of business."

Cassius said nothing.

Aelia arose. "It is time for us to go. You will keep me in touch with Gaius, yes?" Cassius nodded his assent.

As the party re-gathered in the atrium, Aelia pulled Marcus aside. "What do you think, Marcus?"

"I think you have positioned yourself perfectly, Aelia," he said. "I cannot judge whether your donation will influence the Virgins, but you have put wealth in the path of this senator. It is in his interests for you to prevail. Self-interest is a powerful motivator."

She smiled up at him. "You make it sound like a battle."

"Battles are not as bloody as business, but in every way else, they are much the same," he replied.

She kissed him on the cheek. "Let us go and drink some wine. I think there is cause for at least a minor celebration."

* * *

The party arrived back at the domus and sank onto couches in the garden. Rachel and Coventina went to fetch cups and a pitcher of wine. Rachel filled bowls with olives and dates, while Aelia told Demaratus and Flavius what had happened at the meeting. When everyone was assembled, Rachel filled cups of wine and passed them around. Flavius took a long draft of wine, then looked up, puzzled. "Bitter, it is," he said. Coventina took a small sip, spit it out, then leaned over and knocked the wine cup from Aelia's hand, spattering the drink over her dress and onto the couch's pillows.

"What?" Aelia cried out, "how dare...."

"Put down your wine. It is poisoned," ordered Coventina. "Who drank it besides Flavius?"

The rest shook their heads. Demaratus poured his out into a nearby planter. "How much did you drink, brother?" he said to Flavius.

"A cup," said Flavius. "My mouth feels numb."

Marcus jumped up. "I have an antidote that the doctor prepared, I will fetch it."

"Flavius, try to vomit," said Coventina, "I will be right back." She leapt up and ran to her cubiculum.

Flavius knelt near some plants and tried to vomit, putting his finger down his throat, but nothing came out. Rachel knelt and tried to help, but all she could get the optio to eject was some saliva. Flavius began to tremble and his hands stiffened.

Coventina appeared with a small cup of liquid. "Drink this, Flavius. Quickly," she said, pressing it to his lips. Flavius swallowed the potion with difficulty, first choking then heaving up the contents of his stomach. Just then, Marcus returned. "This is mithridatum," said. "You must get this into you."

"Mithridatum is useless," said Coventina, "It is just serves to enrich doctors at the expense of their patients. The only antidote for poison is no poison, and getting it out of Flavius is the first step."

Flavius continued to retch until there was nothing left to throw up. He was sweating and twitching, but gradually his symptoms subsided, leaving him slumped on the garden path. Rachel continued to hold his shoulders.

"What did you give him?" asked Aelia.

"It is a drug that induces vomiting. I think he will recover, but he needs to lie down," answered Coventina.

"Coventina is a healer among her people," said Demaratus, grasping Flavius and lifting him up. Marcus took the other shoulder, and the two men carried Flavius to his bedroom and laid him out on his couch. "I will stay with him," said Rachel.

Coventina had followed them into the room and closely examined the optio. "There is nothing to do but stay with him," she said to Rachel. "If the poison is what I think it is, he may be delirious. He may see things that are not there. Keep him quiet if you can. I will be back in a moment."

Flavius continued to sweat and move restively on the couch. His eyelids fluttered, and he seemed to be looking at nothing, eyes darting about the room. Rachel kept a firm grip on his shoulders and talked softly to him. Coventina returned with a pottery jug and sat down next to the patient. "We must try to get water into him," she said. "That may be difficult because of the drug I gave him, but we have to dilute the poison."

Rachel poured water into a cup. "I will tend to him," she said. Lifting his head, she put the cup to his lips and tipped some water into his mouth. At first, he choked and pushed her away, but he soon seemed to calm down. Before long he began to sip some of the fluid. "I think it best if you all leave," said Rachel. "He is agitated and too many people may be distressing," she said.

"Rachel is right," said Coventina. The Celt put her hand on Rachel's arm, "Let me know if you need help. I will be in the atrium."

Rachel nodded, keeping her grip and her eyes on Flavius.

Marcus, Aelia, Demaratus and Coventina gathered in the atrium. No one said anything for several minutes. "What and who?" the signifer finally asked.

"I suspect the 'what' is Hyoscyamus niger, although it could also be Datura stramonium. You may know them as Henbane and Thorn Apple," said Coventina. "They are both dangerous. As to 'who,' I have no idea, except that it was badly done."

"What do you mean?" asked Marcus.

Coventina sighed. "I hate poison. But if you want to poison someone, you do not use poisons like these. You want something like Amanita phalloides, a mushroom. The symptoms do not appear for almost a day, and by then it is too late. Because this poison's effects are immediate, I could identify it and try to neutralize it. Whoever put this in our wine was not skilled in their craft."

"Thanks to you, we are alive," said Aelia. "We are deeply in your debt, Coventina."

Coventina waved her hand to deflect the praise. "I am a healer, it is what I do," she said simply.

"Will he survive?" asked Marcus.

"Yes," Coventina reassured him. "I caught it in time. He will be ill for a day or so, but he will recover. However, we now have a major problem on our hands."

Demaratus nodded. "This attempt is not likely to be the last. We have to assume that whatever we eat or drink may be poisoned, and the next attempt might be more sophisticated."

"Wait a moment," said Aelia. "Before we discuss what we do, let me assemble the staff." She left and returned minutes later with the staff members, a man and a woman, both whom looked apprehensive.

"Where is Cornelia?" asked Aelia. The staff members looked nervously at one another, and the woman said, "She did not come in today, Lady Dasumi. She left last night saying her mother was ill and she was going to see to her care. She did not return."

Demaratus had retrieved the amphora containing the wine and held it up. "Do you recognize this?" he asked.

The staff nodded. "Yes, sir. But it looks much like the others," the woman said.

"Who brought the wine?" asked the Greek.

"It was delivered," said the man. "We were told it came from a wine merchant, but not told who he was. I would not think to ask that question, sir," the man said, visibly nervous, wiping his hands on his pants.

"Who took the wine from the merchant?" Demaratus asked.

"Cornelia," answered the man.

Aelia dismissed them. "Do you think they are telling the truth?" she asked.

"Does it make any difference?" Marcus replied. "We need to dismiss them and keep all others out of the domus. We will also have to get rid of all our food and wine. We ourselves will have to buy food and drink every day, and from different shops each time."

Coventina nodded. "I agree. We have to be in complete control of everything we eat and drink. It seems clear that the missing staff member is our poisoner, or at least the source of the poisoned wine."

"Do we need a praegustotores?" asked Marcus.

"A taster is a slave," said Rachel.

"I do not think that would be acceptable," Aelia said, glancing at Rachel.

"Of course not," said Marcus looking embarrassed.

"Who did this?" asked Demaratus quietly.

"It is unlikely the Praetorians are behind it. I think they would be far more skilled," said Marcus. "I suspect your brother, Aelia."

"Oh, nothing is past him," agreed Aelia, "and, like most of his schemes, it was badly done."

"Well, we already knew we are being watched. Now we know that someone tried to poison us. We are forewarned," said Demaratus.

XXIV

Julia, and her husband, Lucius, sat with her brother Tiberius Favonius around a small table in the garden of the Aquillius household. Off to one side sat Sabina, Lucius and Julia's daughter, dutifully spinning carded wool into yarn she would then weave. Her brothers, Julius and Sergius, were on an expedition to the Latin Library near the Trajan Forum with their tutor, so the house was quiet.

"We have an opportunity, and we must seize it," said Tiberius. "Our family is well placed with the new emperor. I have allies who have suggested to Decius that I would be a reliable appointment to the Senate. If not the Senate, then maybe a prestigious and lucrative post, like Quaestor."

"And our brother, Marcus, should be appointed to lead that Hispania legion—I forget its name," chimed in Julia.

"The VII Gemina Pia, mother," said Sabina, continuing to spin the wool on a whorl. "Uncle Marcus is acting legate."

"Oh, yes, thank you, Sabina. I can't keep all those names and titles and numbers in my head," said Julia with a small laugh.

Turning to Tiberius she asked, "Have you pressed your friends about Marcus?"

Tiberius hesitated, pouring himself a cup of wine and nibbling on a date. "We can't ask for too much, sister" he said.

"I don't understand," said Julia. "Marcus is a hero. He defeated all those Franks or Goths or whatever. That was a triumph for our family."

"Yes, it was a great accomplishment," said Tiberius, "but we have to think about what is best for our family. If Marcus is appointed legate, he will live in the provinces. Hispania is a long way from Roma, and this city is the Empire's center of power. I wish Marcus well, but there is not much he can do for both our families"—he nodded to Lucius— "in Hispania."

Julia frowned. She found politics confusing. "But can't you be appointed to the Senate or some other post and Marcus also be a..."—she reached for the word, "legate?"

"If we ask for too much, we may get nothing," replied Tiberius. "The point is, what is best for our families? I don't see how Marcus is going to be a help for us here in Roma, and I am certain that our families do not want to move to Hispania."

"No, we do not," said Lucius, his first contribution to the conversation.

"You see, Julia, your family needs to stay here and be protected," said Tiberius, deliberately raising the threat that Philip had posed. That threat had vanished with his death, but it still terrorized his sister.

"I see," said Julia, suddenly looking distressed. "No, we do not want to worry the way we did. I just love Marcus and want him to do well."

"As do I," said Tiberius, "and in the end I think this will come out well for him. And speaking of our family, isn't it time that you were looking to find a suitor for Sabina? I believe she is approaching thirteen, and that is the ideal time for marriage."

"Oh, no, brother, she is still a young girl," protested Julia.

"I would say 'young woman' was a better description," said Tiberius. "Sabina, come sit by us."

"I am fine here, uncle," demurred Sabina, looking intently at the wool she was spinning. She gave him a smile that her eyes belied.

"Have you given thought to marriage, niece?" asked Tiberius.

"I cannot say I have considered it," she replied.

"Well, it is about time you did," said Tiberius. Turning to Julia, he added," I have been giving it some thought, and I have a few matches in mind that would greatly enhance our families' fortunes."

"Oh?" uttered Julia, without enthusiasm.

"Yes," said Tiberius. "I know of a senator who lost his wife last year and is looking to remarry."

"A senator? Aren't they old?" objected Julia.

"This one is not so old. I think he is in his forties. He is quite wealthy and very influential. It would be a catch for Sabina," argued Tiberius.

"I would prefer to catch my own fish, uncle," said Sabina, putting down her yarn.

"That is not your decision, Sabina. It is for your parents to decide such matters, and they need to keep the fortunes of our families in mind," Tiberius declared, a note of annoyance creeping into his voice. "You would have an enormous domus, many slaves, and as much clothes and jewelry as you could want."

"Clothes and jewelry do not interest me, uncle. I like books," she said coldly.

Tiberius turned to Julia, "You have given her too much freedom to do what she wants. She needs to learn the skills of being a good wife and running a household. She won't find that in books."

"Actually, uncle, you can. It's just boring," interjected Sabina.

Tiberius gave her a hostile glare. "What interests you is irrelevant, Sabina. We all have our duties, and yours is to marry well and produce children. You don't even have to be able to read to fulfill those duties."

Sabina said nothing, but her look was unnerving. He expected anger or even fear and uncertainty, not this cold, considered evaluation.

"Well, I leave this matter in your hands, sister. I must be going. There is much work to do if we are to lift up our families," said Tiberius, rising. "I will send you the name of the senator I have in mind."

Julia and Lucius rose as well. Sabina remained seated, but followed him with those disconcerting eyes. Tiberius kissed his sister, nodded to Lucius and directed his parting words to Sabina. "You need to set aside your dolls, Sabina, and take up the role of a proper Roman matron like your mother."

"It was good to see you, uncle. May Fortuna smile on your endeavors," she recited dutifully, returning to her spinning.

Tiberius gathered his cloak and a bag, which he slung across his shoulders, and left, still thinking about Sabina. "Brat," he thought. But the match with Senator Publius Mummius Sisenna would be perfect. The man was rich, influential and, while maybe a little older than he had represented to Julia, exactly the kind of person who could enhance the power and wealth of the Favonius family. Julia may object, but Julia was easily manipulated. In the end, she would do what Tiberius wanted her to do, and Lucius would offer no objection.

"Well, that is a lot to think about, isn't it? said Julia to both Sabina and Lucius. Her husband grunted and poured himself another cup of wine. "He knows what he is doing," he said, then lapsed into silence.

"Sabina, dear?" ventured Julia tentatively.

The girl paused, looking away from her parents, before asking when the family would see Marcus again.

"Oh, I don't know. I will send a note and invite them to dinner," said Julia.

"I will take it," said Sabina rising. "I had meant to visit Marcus and the others in their new domus anyhow."

"Will you be safe?" asked Julia. Tiberius's talk about threats to the family had unnerved her. She had been terrified after the death of her brother Mamercus at the hands of the Praetorians, and all those fears came cascading back.

"Mother, I go to the forum at least three times a week. And I will take Lucretia," said Sabina. Julia's family was not well off enough to purchase a household slave, but she had hired two women, one to do housework, the other to shop and cook. Lucretia was the cook, a stout middle-aged woman who could take care of herself.

"Oh, I suppose that is okay. Just be careful. It is okay, isn't it, Lucius dear?" she asked.

Lucius grunted an assent and poured more wine.

XXV

Julius Dasumi was angry. "We never discussed poison! What were you thinking?" he scolded Gnaeus in a tight voice. The two men were in the same small room sitting around the table. "And it failed? Now they are alerted. I am paying you a fortune for incompetence?"

"You are paying me to kill your sister, Dasumi. How I do it is none of your business," countered Gnaeus. "If you are unhappy, then do it yourself. I will take my expenses and leave."

"Poison?" continued Julius. "And you couldn't get it right? You should be paying me!"

Gnaeus shrugged. "Things go wrong, Dasumi. Maybe not in your life, but for everyone else they do. Why do you think Fortuna's temples are so well endowed? If the poison had worked, I wouldn't need to hire a bunch of expensive muscle. But it didn't."

"In other words. You would have made a bigger profit," hissed Julius.

"Right," said Gnaeus. "You don't try to maximize your profits, Dasumi? Really? Spare me your outrage."

"How dare you talk to me that way," protested Julius, rising.

"I'll talk to you any way I wish, Dasumi. I'm not one of your slaves. Again, if you don't like my methods, find someone else or do it yourself," said Gnaeus dismissively.

Julius mastered his rage. He needed Gnaeus and the man knew it. He took a deep breath. "What do you plan now?" he said at last.

"Your sister's party all went to see her lawyer. They have two bodyguards, plus the three men. I will have nine men waiting and, when they least expect it, we will overwhelm them and you can go back to your province a wealthy man," explained Gnaeus. "Unless, of course, you have decided to take matters into your own hands," he added with just the hint of a sneer.

Gory fantasies of what he would like to do to Gnaeus ran through his head, but Julius kept his voice even. "When?"

"Can't say," replied Gnaeus. "I have the domus under surveillance. I will pull together a team tomorrow. They will stay close, but hidden. When your sister leaves the house, they will get their instructions as to where and when to strike."

Julius stood up. "All right," he said. "Let's hope this works."

"Yeah. You might want to drop by the temple of Fortuna, Dasumi, and make a donation," suggested Gnaeus. He arose, slipped the cloak around his shoulders and left.

Julius stood there for a long time, his mind racing. He sighed. Trying to kill someone is complicated, he thought. Gathering up his small bag, he pulled over his cloak to cover his face and departed. As he walked down the street, a man slipped out of a small café and followed him from a distance.

XXVI

The household was tense, as if preparing for battle. Which, in a sense, it was.

Today was the Festival of Mars Invictus, and Aelia needed to make an appearance. Her lawyer, Cassius Caesenniusa, and Senator Gaius Julius had arranged for her to be at the Tiber for the climax of the event. A procession of Roma's leading officials and major military figures led by the Vestal Virgins would cast thirty Argei into the river, celebrating the three pillars of the Roman Empire—war, agriculture and family. The Senator would stand next to Aelia and point her out to the Virgins, who she hoped would acknowledge her generous donation. The wish was that the contribution would favorably dispose the Virgins toward Aelia.

Marcus was unhappy, but Aelia was adamant. "I must go, I must be at the river, I must be seen," she said, overriding his worries about security. "This is why we are here, Marcus."

He made one last try. "Aelia, we have survived one attempt at our lives. I do not think it will be the last. We have to take everyone. We can't provide security in two places, and Flavius has only just recovered from his poisoning." The optio insisted he was fine, but he looked pale and drawn. But there was no moving Aelia. "I intend to be at the Tiber when the procession arrives, Marcus. I hope you will be there with me," she said.

Marcus was not used to being dismissed. Since he had become legate, he had become used to being the one who dismissed people, not the other way around. But he also recognized the tone in Aelia's voice that meant the discussion was over.

Giving in to the inevitable, Marcus called the security team together. The men—Demaratus, Flavius and himself, plus Vilaus and Numerius—would form a ring around the women. But the streets would be crowded, and the ring would have to be tight for it to move through the crowds. That meant that Aelia would be only a few feet away from any potential assassin.

All the men armed themselves with swords. Demaratus also strapped his Damascus blade to his thigh, and Marcus slipped his pugio under his cloak. Marcus wore his bronze breastplate, and Flavius and Demaratus their chain shirts. While a bronze breastplate would turn aside most swords, chain would not stop a determined assassin.

The party started early—the streets would soon be made impassable by the multitudes watching the procession—and arrived successfully at the steps of the Portico of Octavia near the river. The senator was waiting for them and made space for Aelia on the steps next to himself. Marcus had trouble setting the security where he thought it would be most effective because others had already commandeered the temple stairs, but he eventually managed to provide cover for Aelia on three sides. When he tried to stand to her front, closing the cordon, she shooed him away. "They have to see me, Marcus, I want them to put a face on my donation," she said, pulling him to her side. He was not happy about being pushed and ordered about, but it was not the time or place for an argument.

It was growing warm, and there was no shade. Marcus's breastplate trapped the heat, and the sweat rolled off him. In their chain, Flavius and Demaratus looked more comfortable, but after an hour of standing in the hot sun, no one was particularly happy. Gradually, the sound of drums grew louder and the procession, led by several men carrying a statue of Mars, eventually came into view. Behind them were six young women, the Vestal Virgins, and a string of officials. The Virgins were followed by men dressed in military garb who danced, stopping at one point to sing a hymn.

"Salii," whispered Flavius to Rachel and Coventina when they looked at him for an explanation. Singing, dancing soldiers was not something they had ever encountered before. "They are priests, but dress as soldiers for the ceremony. Behind them are Augures, Haruspices, Flamines and Arvals, all different kinds of priests."

The priests were followed by military leaders, including tribunes and legates. Marcus recognized Quintus Pompeius, his old commander from Britannia, commander of the Vigiles, and now a senator. Behind the military men came others carrying straw men, bound hand and foot.

"What are those?" whispered Coventina to Flavius.

"Argei," he whispered back.

"What do they mean?" asked Rachel.

"I don't know," admitted Flavius. "I have heard many

explanations. Some say they represent a time when our ancestors sacrificed people to insure our crops. Others say the meaning is lost, but it is an integral part of the ceremony."

"I thought this was about Mars and war," said Coventina.

"It is, but other things as well. The procession also celebrates Quirinus. He was an ancient king and is associated with agriculture," said Flavius, "and the Virgins sanctify the Roman family."

The procession was approaching the temple steps, and the senator put his arms around Aelia's shoulders and bowed his head to them, indicating Aelia. The lead Virgin acknowledged the bow and smiled at Aelia, who curtsied and gave her a dazzling smile in return. The procession passed by, headed for the river. It was hard to see much from where they stood, but eventually the Argei were passed forward and the virgins and the priests stood facing the Tiber. After a series of chants and prayers—the people on the temple steps were too far away to catch more than an occasional word—the Argei were thrown into the river and the procession began to disperse. Many people headed for the Flavian Amphitheatre, where games would soon start up.

Senator Gaius smiled down at Aelia. "I think that went well, Aelia. You were acknowledged by the head Virgin."

"Thank you, senator. You have been most helpful. When should we meet again?" she asked.

"It depends on what your brother is up to. The Senate will not be in session for the next three days because of the festival and the games. I will keep you informed," he told her.

"And your plan?" she asked.

He smiled and pointed to his ears. "Let us keep that a secret," he said. Then, with a short bow, he turned and headed off into the crowd.

Marcus sidled up to her. "We should wait a bit, Aelia. Let the crowds thin out. That will make for better security."

"Do you really think we would be attacked in broad daylight during a festival?" she asked.

"I don't know," he said. "So we should play it safe."

She sighed. "All right, but I want to get home and bathe. Being in Roma is like living in a dirty steam bath."

A half hour later the crowds had largely dispersed, and the party began to retrace its steps, looking for mostly deserted back streets, skirting plazas where people still amassed. The security bubble widened out, and the three women chatted at its center.

Suddenly Rachel stopped. "Flavius, we are under attack!"

For a moment none of the others did anything, but Flavius turned, faced the outside of the ring, and drew his gladis.

"What are you talking about?" asked Aelia, "I don't...." She cut her sentence short. They were surrounded on all sides by a group of men converging on them.

Marcus spied two men headed for him, each armed with a short sword. He whipped out his gladis and pugio and attacked, throwing both assailants off balance. They were not used to being attacked by their intended victims. This slowed them down, allowing Marcus to drive his sword into the thigh of one man and hold off the second with his pugio. Out of the corner of his eye, he saw two men attacking Flavius, who was keeping them off balance with a combination of small retreats and quick advances. It was clear that their assailants were not soldiers, who know that when under attack you don't fall back, but advance instead, thereby throwing off the attackers' timing and coordination.

Flavius quickly analyzed what he was up against. He faced two men armed with swords and converging on him from two sides. The solution was to isolate and defeat them one by one. He moved to his left to draw the attention of one attacker, forcing him to slow up, then quickly pivoted to his right to attack the man's left side, driving him toward the other assailant. The effect was that one attacker partially shielded him from the other. And while his first target was trying to get around the other man, Flavius struck, clashing swords with his right hand and driving his pugio up at the man's chest with his left. The attack was not wholly successful, but he did bloody the man, who fell back, bumping his fellow assailant. Flavius pounced. Never let the enemy catch his breath and reorganize.

Demaratus glanced to his right where Vilaus and Numerius each confronted a man, then shifted his attention to the giant advancing on him. Demaratus quickly gauged the situation. The man was huge, but probably not very quick. But the most pressing question was where were the assassins who were sure to be aiming for Aelia? He stepped to his left and slashed at the man in front of him, who backed off briefly and then charged.

Just then he saw—or rather felt—movement to his right and marked two men emerging from a door, heading for the women. He wanted to confront them, but the man in front of him attacked again. It was a well-laid ambush. While security was fighting off their attackers, two assassins went after Aelia.

On paper, battles are always perfectly choreographed. This ambush certainly was. Its object was not to kill everyone in the party, just to keep the security busy enough that it couldn't come to the aid of the target. And in the opening minutes of the assault that is exactly what happened. But the best designed battle plan can't protect against two things—the unexpected and bad luck.

And Gneaus Domitius's battle plan encountered both.

The two assassins slipped by Numerius on their left and Demaratus on their right and headed straight for Aelia, brushing aside the other two women in their path.

That was when they met the unexpected.

One man shoved Coventina aside to strike at Aelia, only to find the woman clinging to his sword arm. Annoyed, he tried to pull back his sword to strike her, but she moved inside and hugged him closely, so he could not free his sword. Surprising him with her strength, she brought her knee up right between his legs. A sharp pain coursed through him, and he shoved her away hard with his left hand.

It was then that he realized he was in trouble. The woman had a knife, which she drove upwards into his chest, then bit deeply into his cheek. He screamed, pushing her away as he tried to back up, but she clung to his sword arm, slashing at him with the knife. Finally, he spun her around, only to feel a stinging sensation at his back. Aelia had driven a knife into him. His knees buckled, and he fell slowly forward on his face.

The second assassin was driving toward Aelia, when Rachel stepped in his way. He stabbed at her with his sword, but she turned aside, and he failed to make contact. Instead of running, as he'd expected, she circled him, grasped his neck in her arms and pulled sharply backwards. She was strong, and the weight of her body threw him off balance. He tried thrusting the sword backwards, but she clung to him so tightly that he couldn't angle the blade to strike her.

And then bad luck struck.

Flavius had wounded one of his attackers, who had backed off, but the optio was tiring. The aftereffects of the poison were making themselves felt. Seeing Flavius flag, the other man pressed his attack and drove his sword into Flavius's side. Drawing back for the coup de grace, he caught his foot on the leg of his fellow assailant and stumbled back, falling hard on the cobblestones.

Flavius turned to see Rachel's attacker finally free himself and pull back for a killing thrust that he never got to complete. Flavius drove his sword so deeply into the man's back that it came out his chest. The man fell without a sound. Next to him lay the attacker Aelia and Coventina had fought off.

And with that the attack was over. The men assaulting Marcus, Demaratus, Flavius and his cousins had all backed off. They had been hired to assassinate a woman, not to fight the battle of Cannae. This was supposed to be a quick kill followed by a swift exit. Instead, two were dead and two wounded. The team of attackers melted away.

The three women huddled together, their backs to one another, Aelia and Coventina extending their knife arms. The men did the same. "Is everyone all right?" asked Marcus.

"Flavius is wounded," said Rachel. A stain was spreading on Flavius's left side, and blood was running down his leg into his boots.

"I'm alright," said Flavius. "I've had worse."

"You are weakened by the poison, Flavius. Sit and let Coventina look at it," urged Rachel. When Flavius started to protest, she stamped her foot. "Sit down!"

He sat, and Coventina lifted his mail shirt. She used her knife to slash material from her dress, and cut a long ribbon of wool. She bunched the material in the wound and then wrapped it tightly with the wool ribbon. "We need a litter," she said.

"I can walk," protested Flavius.

"You can also bleed to death, optio. But not while I am around. We need a litter," said Coventina.

"I'll get one" said Vilaus, and went off in the direction of a forum.

Rachel knelt by Flavius. "Thank you," she said.

"No need. You seemed to be doing just fine," he said with a grin.

"No, I was going to die if you had not come to my rescue," she said. Then leaning forward, she kissed him. "Now lie down and be still." Flavius's face had turned bright red, but it did not appear to be wound-related.

Marcus stood over the two assassins. "They did not expect that you women would also take up arms against them, and they paid for their short-sightedness," he said.

Demaratus slipped his knife back into his thigh scabbard. "No plan survives contact with the enemy. At least this enemy" he said, indicating Rachel, Coventina and Aelia.

A crowd had begun to gather. "Can we help?" asked a man in a leather work apron.

"Only one of us is wounded, and we sent for a litter," said

Marcus, "but if you could keep the crowd back that would be helpful."

The man with the apron grabbed a younger man by the shoulder, and the two of them created a perimeter. "Shameful," one woman said, "and on such an important day." Another woman asked, "Who are these men?" pointing at the two dead assassins.

"We don't know," said Marcus. He turned one of the dead men over. "Do you recognize either of them?" he asked the crowd.

Some in the crowd pressed forward and a number of cross conversations broke out. "I have seen that one near the docks," one woman said, pointing to the man Coventina and Aelia had killed, "But I don't know his name."

"Were they trying to rob you?" asked an older man.

Aelia suddenly realized she had a stage. She seized it. Stepping forward, her stolla flecked with blood, she answered the man. "No, they were trying to kill us," she said. Pointing to Marcus, she went on, "This is Marcus Favonius, Legate of the VII Legion from Hispania, the legion which defeated a Frankish invader three times its size and liberated the city of Tarraco, founded by the great Scipio. Our wounded comrade is his second-in-command. This assassination attempt is a mark of shame on our glorious Empire."

The crowd growled its agreement. "Disgraceful," one man shouted, while another asked, "Where are the Vigiles?"

Aelia had the attention of the crowd and she did not waste it. Holding up her knife, its blade stained with blood, and throwing her arm around Coventina, she said, "We do not need the Vigiles. This woman and I killed one assassin, and my sister

Rachel helped fell the other. We women of Hispania know how to defend ourselves."

The crowd applauded. Rachel and Coventina looked embarrassed. But the little speech had fired up the audience. "That little slip of a girl," said one man, pointing at Aelia, "killed an assassin," and two women said, "Such courage," indicating Coventina. "So big, and with red hair," another said, "she must be a Celt."

The effect was exactly what Aelia wanted—a friendly crowd surrounding the party, ensuring that the attack would not be renewed. Her speech would get repeated in the fora all over the city, adding another layer of protection against a future assault.

Within minutes Vilaus returned, trailed by four men carrying a door. They lifted Flavius onto it, and the party headed off to the domus, followed by some of the crowd. They arrived at their destination accompanied by almost a hundred people, who milled around outside until the Vigiles showed up and got them to disperse.

XXVII

Flavius flinched as Coventina removed the temporary bandage she had put on his wound following the attack. She examined it critically. "I will need warm water and a piece of my luggage, a small, red leather case." she said to Rachel, who left swiftly to retrieve them.

Flavius looked down at his side. "I've had worse," he said.

"Maybe, but this is bad enough. The bleeding has pretty much stopped, but I need to clean the wound and re-dress it," she told him. Rachel appeared with a bronze bowl, a wash cloth and small satchel. Coventina took the bowl and carefully began to cleanse the wound. "I will need to stitch this," she said, almost to herself. Turning to the red case, she opened it and began laying out needles, a small scissors, ointments, and some clean bandages. "Rachel," she said looking up, "I will need some linen and long strips of wool. Can you get them for me?"

Coventina opened a small packet and took out several strands of thin silk and a needle. She also withdrew a bottle and partially emptied its contents into a wine cup. She added a small amount of water to the cup, stirred it, and tipped Flavius's head forward.

"Drink this, optio. It will make you feel better." Flavius dutifully drank the cup down.

"What was that?" he asked.

"An extract of poppy seeds. It will dampen the pain," she explained, adding. "This will hurt."

"I'll be fine," said Flavius.

"Men," said Coventina quietly, shaking her head. She threaded the needle with a strand of silk and tied a small knot. Then she carefully joined the edges of the wound and began stitching them together. She moved quickly, and the dribble of blood soon stopped. After more than a dozen stitches, she carefully tied off the silk and gently washed the wound once more. Reaching into her bag, she pulled out a jar of ointment, which she slathered on the area. When Flavius looked at her questioningly, "Colostrum, made from mother's milk. It is useful for keeping gangrene from developing."

"Aye, that's bad stuff," said Flavius. He was exhausted. The shock of the wound, the loss of blood, the poppy seed mixture, and the stitches—on top of his weakened condition from the attempted poisoning—were taking a toll.

"I think you will be all right, Flavius. The wound was clean, and I got to it early. But a prayer to one of your gods would do no harm. I have called upon my own, but we are a long way from where they live," said Coventina, putting a linen bandage on the sutures. She sat Flavius up briefly, just long enough to wrap the wool strips around his trunk to secure the bandage.

Flavius nodded. "I have made a pledge to Vejovis, the god of healing," he said. And with that he lay down, looking pale and drawn.

"I will sit with him, Coventina," said Rachel, moving her chair closer to the patient's couch.

"Watch the wound. If the stain spreads, call me," she instructed. She arose, patted Flavius on the forehead and left.

"How do you feel? asked Rachel.

"Uh, like I am floating," he answered. "Coventina's poppy seeds, I guess. But good. I will be up in no time."

"You will get up when Coventina says you can get up," said Rachel firmly. "You have a bad wound."

"Well, I won't argue with you, Rachel. I caught a glimpse of you hanging on to that assassin," said Flavius. "I don't think it's a good idea to pick a fight with the likes of you."

Rachel smiled down at him. "You saved me, Flavius," she said softly.

"It's my job," he said simply,

"Men," she said. "Why is it so difficult for you to accept a simple compliment?"

"Uh, well, I'm not sure," he answered weakly. "It was... well, I saw you hanging on to that bastard, and it just scared me to death. You know, I, ah..." he trailed off.

Rachel looked down at him and said softly, "Yes?"

"I, uh," Flavius stumbled on, "I was so afraid you might be hurt. You see, I like you a lot." The last sentence was rushed and breathless, a product of his injury, his shyness, and the poppies.

"I like you a lot, too, Flavius," said Rachel, "and we should talk about this when you are feeling stronger."

"Yes, I would like that," he said.

Rachel paused and put her hand on his chest. "I am not an easy person, Flavius. And our worlds have been very different."

"You are under the impression that I am an easy person?" he asked with a weak smile.

She smiled back at him. "I find you much more complex and interesting than you portray yourself. That is attractive. But I warn you there are complexities that you might not be aware of. When I was freed, I became a citizen of the Empire, but I am not a Roman."

"Demaratus explained some of this to me," said Flavius. "I will do whatever needs to be done, and I don't care how long it takes," he said. "Well, I mean I care, but I will be patient," he said, a little color coming back into his cheeks. "Just tell me what to do."

"Not now, Flavius. You need to rest," she said with a smile. "Sleep and we will talk later."

He protested that there was no way he could sleep, then promptly began to snore. Rachel looked carefully at the wound, then drew a blanket over him and sat quietly in the dim room. "Life is going to get complicated," she thought.

* * *

Coventina retired to the atrium, where the rest of the party, minus Vilaus and Numerius, were seated. "How is he?" asked Marcus, rising as she entered.

"I think he will be fine," said Coventina, "but one can never tell with wounds. He has lost some blood and he is still weakened from the poison, but Flavius is strong." Glancing around the room she asked, "What of the rest of you?"

Marcus and Demaratus were both unmarked. "They were not

interested in us," said Marcus. "They just wanted to neutralize us so as to assassinate Aelia."

"I agree," said Demaratus. "They did not press their attack and broke it off as soon as it became obvious that the assassination attempt had failed."

"And it failed because they did not take into account our women," said Marcus with a chuckle.

"Our women?" said Aelia, arching an eyebrow and putting her hands on her hips.

"I didn't mean it in that way," protested Marcus, "I meant, uh...." He reached for words, failing to find any.

Aelia laughed. "Men are so easily teased," she said. "We are alive because we all worked together. My sister held off one attacker by hugging him, and Coventina killed the other right off. And you men were outnumbered but held them at bay. I am concerned for Flavius, but I thought we were rather grand today. I would love to see the expression on my brother's face when he gets the news that his second attempt to kill me was more of a debacle than his first."

"It may not be his last," said Marcus. "We beat off that assassination today, but it could have gone the other way. Their plan was actually quite good and would probably have worked on anyone but us."

"We must stay vigilant," agreed Demaratus. "But it will be harder to do what they tried today. News of the fight and how a group of assassins were defeated by three women will get out. You saw the way the crowd reacted. I think we have enhanced Aelia's chances with the Senate."

"I think you are right, signifer," said Marcus. "We need to hire some runners and post this news on acta diurnas throughout the city."

"Acta diurnas?" asked Coventina.

"Public announcement boards," answered Marcus, "they are all over the city. We can write up something and have it posted by the runners. I will compose it."

"I have papyrus," said Aelia. "Maybe Vilaus and Numerius can find us some runners."

"I will talk with them," said Demaratus, heading for the front door.

Within hours the news had spread.

* * *

"I was willing to ignore your incompetence with poison, Gnaeus, but it is apparent that you are incompetent in all things," hissed Julius.

"The plan would have worked if it were not for those women," said Gnaeus mildly. "Your sister is a dangerous person, Dasumi, considerably more so than you."

"How dare you!" Julius shouted. "You charge me a fortune and bungle every attempt."

"I will not ask for full payment, Dasumi. Half will do," said Gnaeus.

Gnaeus sat at the small table in the small room, while Julius stalked back and forth, his face flushed, his fists balled.

"You will get nothing!" said Julius. "I do not pay for failure."

"Hmm," said Gnaeus, examining his fingernails. "Let me explain something, Dasumi. If you fail to pay me what I ask—and I am giving you a break—I will make sure the authorities know about this. Ordinarily, one need not fear the Vigiles, but I have learned that its commander is an old Army comrade of Marcus Favonius. You would be charged with attempted murder of a family member, a crime that is especially frowned upon. Do you know what they will do to you, Dasumi? The punishment is the poena cullel. They will sew you into a bag with a dog, a snake, a rooster and a monkey and throw you into the Tiber. I am told it is a most uncomfortable way to die."

"You wouldn't dare! They would take you as well as me," said Julius.

"I think not, Dasumi. You see, I have a special relationship with the Vigiles. I 'contribute' to them and they make sure I am well protected. You, on the other hand, being a provincial, have no such standing, As I said, half of what you owe me will be sufficient," said Gnaeus quietly.

"You have made me a laughing stock!" shouted Julius.

"You are a self-made man, Dasumi, but you had best keep your voice down unless you want to get overly intimate with several animals. Now, the money you owe?" insisted Gnaeus.

Julius had turned scarlet red, but reached into his cloak, counted out 25 golden aureas and flung them on the table.

"Nice doing business with you, Dasumi," said Gnaeus, gathering in the coins.

* * *

Aeilus Hadrianus, legate of the Praetorian Guard looked up at his tribune, Antonius Clodius. He pointed to a papyrus sheet in front of him. "Is this true?" he asked.

The tribune shrugged his shoulders. "Who knows? But I do

know it is a subject of much conversation in the streets. I heard it myself from the aide I sent to take this from an acta diurnas."

Aeilus leaned back in his chair. "If there is any truth to this, Antonius, then we need to rethink things."

"Yes, sir. The thought occurred to me as well. This Marcus Favonius is suddenly a popular hero," he said.

"Girls?" said the legate.

"If the rumors are true, the women killed two of the assassins. The men merely drove off their attackers. Not girls to be trifled with, it seems," said Antonius with a grin. "Maybe we should get some of them to take on the Goths."

"And this farce was organized by the woman's brother?" continued Aeilus.

"We don't know that for certain, but this Dasumi has been meeting with Gnaeus Domitius, and the assassins were his men. Shall I have the Vigiles look into it, sir?" asked the tribune.

The legate laughed. "I doubt there is anything the authorities could do to him that would be worse than this humiliation. Being bagged up with a monkey and drowned in the Tiber might be a relief."

"Indeed," chuckled the tribune. "This will not be an easy one to live down. But the matter of the will is still before the Senate and the emperor is due to leave the city within days."

The legate rose and began to pace. "What have you found about the matter concerning the Franks and Tarraco? How did their army get all the way to Hispania without anyone trying to stop it?"

"Uh, sir, are we finished with this Favonius matter?" asked Antonius, suddenly confused.

"They are related," answered Aeilus.

"They are?" wondered the tribune.

"Yes. What did you find?" said the legate.

"That the legion in Norbo was instructed not to impede their passage. I have not received any firm evidence about other legions in Gaul, but it is hard to come to any other conclusion than that there was a decision to allow the Franks to pass," said Antonius. "But I don't see...Oh!"

"Right, tribune. Who was the commander of the VII Legion that defeated the Franks? Marcus Favonius," said Aeilus. "Why would the legions in Gaul stand aside? Because they wanted the VII Legion destroyed. Why destroyed? Because the VII has earned its name 'pia' by being loyal to the Empire. Correct?" asked the legate.

"I guess," said Antonius tentatively.

"If you were going to set up a separate empire in Gaul, you would have to be sure that the legions under your command were loyal. If you weren't certain about their loyalty, the easiest thing to do is to eliminate them," explained Aeilus.

"You think that is what is going on?" queried the tribune.

"I can't think of another explanation, can you?" challenged the legate. Not waiting for an answer, he continued. "There have been rumors of a 'Gaulish empire' for some time, and that would be bad for the Empire, Antonius. If something is bad for the Empire, it is bad for the Praetorian Guard. And you and I, tribune, are the Praetorian Guard. If Marcus Favonius and the VII Legion are loyal to the Empire—and given that they were set up to be attacked by the enemies of the Empire, we can assume that is the case—then, ipso facto, Marcus Favonius is an ally of the Guard. Rather than bringing him harm, we should ensure he is appointed legate."

The tribune was silent for a time. "We are going to use our influence to ensure that a man we tried to assassinate two years ago, and whose family killed a comrade of ours, is appointed the legate of a legion?" he finally asked.

"Correct," said Aeilus. "The world is a complicated place, tribune."

XXVIII

Rachel opened the door to find Sabina, flanked by a stout older woman.

"Is Flavius well? And did you really you really strangle that assassin to death?" Sabina asked.

Rachel gave her a warm smile. "Sabina and Lucretia, how nice to see you again. Please come in. I will fetch Marcus. And, no, I did not strangle him. I just clung to him. Flavius killed him. And Flavius received a serious wound, but he is healing."

"Really?" said Sabina, stepping into the atrium. "You held onto this man who was trying to kill you? I would love to have seen that."

"He was trying to kill Aelia, I just got in the way," said Rachel.

"Isn't that what our legions do? Get in the way of people trying to kill us?" She shook her head and clasped her hands, her eyes glowing. "It was wonderful. Marcus wrote to me about you and Aelia and how you fought the Mori, but I thought he might be exaggerating. Now I will rebuke him for understatement."

Rachel laughed. "Please do not. It was the VII Legion who saved us in Mauretania."

"Oh, men always get the credit, but where would they be without us?" Sabina asked, but it was not really a question that required an answer. Rachel left to fetch Marcus, and Lucretia quietly slipped into the garden, taking a bench in a shaded corner.

Sabina occupied herself by examining the frescoes until Marcus appeared. He greeted her with a hug and a kiss. "It is a delight to see you, niece."

"I am here on business, uncle. Can we find a quiet place to talk?" Sabina said, sounding very adult.

"Of course, Sabina, please come with me," he said, puzzled. He led her to the small library and closed the door. "Now what is this about, niece?"

"Your brother Tiberius is not your friend, uncle," said Sabina.

Marcus was silent for a moment. This was not a conversation one held with a child, but then he didn't think of Sabina as a child. Indeed, he looked forward to her letters filled with intelligent observations about politics. "Why do you say that?" he asked.

"My uncle Tiberius is positioning himself for higher office in Roma, Uncle Marcus, and you are a problem," she told him.

It was an amazing statement coming from someone who was still twelve. "Positioning himself?" That was not a formulation he had expected from a person as young as Sabina. "Sit, Sabina, and tell me more about this," said Marcus.

Sabina repeated the conversation between her mother and uncle, adding that she was supposed to be at the market by the forum, so her time was limited. "It was something I thought you needed to know, uncle," she said.

Marcus smiled. "Tiberius has always limited his definition of the family to himself. What is good for him is good for us all. This does not surprise me, but it is an important piece of information. For one thing, it means that confiding in my brother would be folly."

Sabina nodded. "It was painful to listen to, uncle. I confess I do not always understand adults."

"Niece, you are an adult, and one with considerably better observation powers than most people three times your age. I am sorry you had to hear that," he added.

"I am not," she said. "It is certainly more interesting than playing with dolls. But I am in some difficulty and would appreciate your advice."

"Of course, Sabina. What concerns you?" asked Marcus.

Sabina smoothed her stolla. "Your brother wishes to marry me off to some senator who he says is wealthy and influential, attributes that draw Tiberius like a flame draws moths," she said.

Marcus laughed. "Do I have your permission to repeat that line to Aelia? It is very much the way she talks. I promise it will not go beyond that."

Sabina nodded her assent and then persisted in her request for advice, "My difficulty?"

Marcus grew serious. "The problem is that it is your father who makes the decisions on matters like your marriage. And frankly, I do not know Lucius very well."

"I love my father, but there is not much to know," she acknowledged. "In any case, he would not do anything my mother did not agree with. My mother may seem scattered and shallow, but inside she is made of steel and my father knows it."

"Hmm," said Marcus, leaning back. "Sabina, we need to include Aelia in this conversation."

"If you think that would be helpful," she said.

"Let me fetch her," said Marcus.

While Marcus was gone, Sabina wandered around the library pulling out books and scrolls and skimming through some of them. She was particularly taken with one that featured drawings of birds, some of which she had never seen before. Finally, Marcus, trailing Aelia, re-entered the room. The two women embraced and spent several minutes talking about the assassination attempt and what people were saying about it—the general consensus being that it was the work of her brother. It was the kind of gossip on which Roma dwellers thrived.

After a slight pause, Aelia asked, "How would you feel about leaving Roma, Sabina?"

The girl considered this for a bit. "I love this city, Aelia. Where would I go?"

"You would live with me, Sabina, and with your uncle when he is around," she said. "The VII Legion is based in a rather cold and dreary place in the north. Corduba, where I live, is warm and lovely. And from what he tells me, you have a head for politics. That means you have a head for business."

"But how would this happen?" asked Sabina.

"Aelia would talk to your mother, Sabina. And frankly, Aelia can talk a snake out of his skin," said Marcus.

Aelia gave him a sidelong glance, then added, "Men are easy to influence."

Sabina hesitated. "Yes, but I would miss Roma."

"This offer is contingent on what happens with my father's

will, Sabina," said Aelia. "If it is overturned, I will lose all my resources."

"That won't happen," said Sabina. "You are considered a hero, Aelia, and not even an emperor will go against a hero, particularly not an emperor who has just ascended to the throne."

Aelia laughed. "She is, indeed, a political animal, Marcus. I hope she is right."

"I am rarely wrong on these matters," said Sabina, "but will I have to marry in Hispania?"

"Not if you don't wish to, my dear. I am not married and do quite well," said Aelia. "If you marry, all your property goes to your husband. It is better to remain single and have your man visit."

Marcus was uncomfortable with this advice, but kept his tongue.

Sabina nodded. "That sounds like fun, I agree. But I should be returning home." She hugged and kissed Marcus, and then turned to Aelia. "You will emerge triumphant tomorrow, Aelia, if for no other reason than that the senators will be afraid to anger you."

After Sabina and Lucretia left, Aelia turned to Marcus. "Your niece is truly amazing," she said. "I would love to have her in Corduba."

"What will you say to my sister?" he asked.

Aelia waved her hand dismissively. "Oh, that she will become wealthy and influential, that kind of thing. I suspect the 'wealth' part will be well received. I will suggest that you become her guardian. If she agrees and gets her husband to go along, no one could force her to make a marriage agreement for Sabina without your permission. So, what do you think about her prediction?"

"She is insightful, Aelia, and she loves Senate politics," he said. "It was the subject of most of her letters. She has good instincts about what people think. She spends much of her time at the market talking with people rather than shopping. I suspect what she says is accurate. The question is, will the emperor act on it?"

"Speaking of which, we need to prepare, my love. My lawyer is coming to visit this afternoon," she said. "As a woman, I cannot attend the debate at the curia, but you and Demaratus can."

"We will be there," he assured her.

"And the senators must know who you are," she said thoughtfully. "I will make sure Senator Gaius Julius points you out. We have much to do."

XXIX

It was early in the afternoon, but the Curia in the Imperial Forum was beginning to fill with senators when Marcus and Demaratus arrived. While in theory there were 600 members of the body, it was rare that more than a hundred attended with any regularity. But the times were uncertain, and what with Emperor Decius preparing to go north to face the Goths, more than the usual number of senators were expected.

The comitium surrounding the Curia, where the public gathered to hear speeches—or to give them—was filling up. News that the Senate would take up an issue that involved a prominent army commander had filtered out. And there was the attempted assassination of that commander. There were no seats for spectators in the Curia, so those eager to see the proceedings clustered along the two side walls of the Senate chamber. Space was limited, but Marcus and Demaratus had arrived early enough to secure a spot.

Customarily, the emperor would have presided over the assembly, but he was occupied with organizing the expedition and had sent his youngest son, Hostilian, to act in his place.

The young man, flanked by two consuls, was seated facing the senators, but the body had not yet been called to order. Groups of senators conferred with one another, and Marcus pointed out Julius, huddled with two senators, to Demaratus.

"The snake is here?" exclaimed Demaratus. "We should cut his throat."

"Violence is not allowed in the Senate, signifer, and it would not do our cause any good," said Marcus. "Senator Gaius Julius says he has a plan."

The senator, who was conversing with two of his colleagues, glanced back at Marcus and Demaratus. While some of the senators were aware that there was a dispute over the Dasumi will, few knew the particulars. Moreover, word was out that the target of an assassination attempt would be present at the meeting. In short, it looked like it was going to be an interesting session. That had drawn senators who would ordinarily have been happy to sit at home in their gardens, so attendance was high. There was nothing like scandal and intrigue to get the senators into the Curia. The Senate had held the major decision-making power during the Republic, but in the Empire power resided with the emperor. Yet when times were uncertain, that could change.

At one point Julius scanned the crowd and noted that Marcus and Demaratus were in attendance. The latter caught his eye because the Greek was staring at him. He shuddered. The last time he had encountered Demaratus, the Greek had threatened to disembowel him if anything happened to Aelia. Nothing had, but not for lack of trying, and he wondered if Demaratus remembered the threat. The signifer's cold stare suggested he did.

He would have to surround himself with the security he had hired following the botched assassination attempt.

Julius turned back to the two senators in his party—Publius Acilius, the senior of the trio who had met with Julius, was feeling ill and was not in attendance—and asked, "What is the plan?"

"Senator Avidius Cassius will introduce the proposal to overturn the will after the current business is done. We have talked with several other senators, and they have agreed to vote with us," said Lucius Minicius.

"They should," grumbled Julius, "it has cost me enough."

"Wealth requires investment," Avidius pointed out.

"Well, I leave the matter in your hands," Julius said sourly.

"There may be a problem," whispered Lucius.

"What?" protested Julius. "I thought I had put out enough money to get rid of problems."

"The attack on your sister has generated sympathy, even among the senators," explained Avidius. "How that will affect the discussion is not clear."

"Why would an attempted robbery affect a vote in the Senate?" countered Julius.

Both men looked at him. "'Attempted robbery?' In broad daylight? And by chance your sister was the target? Who would believe that?" scoffed Lucius.

"I had nothing to do with it," whispered Julius through clenched teeth.

"Yes, well, the Senate is about to come to order, so you need to find a place to watch the proceedings," said Lucius, dismissing

Julius, who turned and made his way to the wall opposite Marcus and Demaratus.

Hostilian arose and called the senators to order. By now there were well over 200, and they took their seats in rows that ringed one side of the Curia. For the next three hours, senators held forth on taxes, the need to upgrade the sewers, and problems with water storage. Dozens of senators left the Curia, some to return, others to go home, having had enough for the day. Marcus and Demaratus shifted restlessly, noticeably uncomfortable from standing for hours in uniform.

"Romans can talk," grumbled Demaratus.

"I thought it was you Greeks who taught us rhetoric?' said Marcus with a smile.

"We never imagined that you would use it to bore people to death," whispered Demaratus.

Marcus jostled his arm. "That is one of the senators that Julius is speaking with. I think the play is about to begin."

Senator Avidius Cassius arose and indicated he wished to speak, but before he was recognized Senator Gaius Julius also indicated he wanted the floor.

Avidius protested. "I asked to speak first, Honorable Hostilian," he said.

"But I am senior," said Gaius, "and I ask the chair to uphold the rules of our body. The senior senator has first right to speak."

Hostilian looked confused and huddled with the two consuls before finally ruling that, as the senior senator, Gaius did have first right to speak. Avidius glared at Gaius, but took his seat.

"I wish to raise a most grievous issue," said Gaius. "It is the matter of grain." Stopping for a moment, he pulled out a long scroll. "I have here the records on grain shipments from Gaul, Egypt and Mauretania." He then began listing tonnages from all three provinces for each month of the last year. When he finished with that, Avisius rose to speak. "Senator," said Gaius coldly, "I am not done. Please be so good as to sit down until I am finished." Avisius sent him a poisonous look, but, again, sat down.

"Now let us compare last year's grain tonnages to this year's," he said. He continued to drone on for almost an hour. When he had finished with the comparison, Avisius again arose to speak, but Gaius said, "I am not finished, Senator. Besides grain, there is also the matter of wool." At that, some of the senators began laughing.

"What is going on?" whispered Demaratus.

Marcus grinned. "It is a filibuster, signifer."

"A what?" he asked.

"It is the rule of the Senate that you cannot interrupt a senator while he is talking. Cato the Younger used the filibuster to thwart Caesar on a number of occasions. Gaius Julius is preventing Julius's senator from speaking," he explained.

"But he can't talk forever," said Demaratus.

"He doesn't have to," said Marcus. "He only has to talk until it begins to get dark. The Senate must adjourn at dusk."

By this time, Gaius had moved on from wool to marble imports, and many of the senators began gathering their belongings and heading for the exit. Demaratus pointed to Julius, who strode back and forth, his face flushed with rage. "The mills of the Gods grind slowly, sir, but they grind most fine."

Marcus chuckled. "I wonder what he spent to come up with nothing?"

"Is it over?" asked Demaratus.

"Not quite," said Marcus. "The emperor has been petitioned. He could decide in Julius's favor or do nothing and let the Vestal Virgins decide the matter."

Eventually both consuls leaned in to Hostilian and whispered to him. The young man looked relieved. He had been trying to remain awake during the long lists of grain tonnage, wool shipments, and marble imports, and now Gaius had shifted to the import of exotic animals for the games. "Senator Gaius Julius Cornutus. We are fascinated by your insightful speech on, ah, various things, but I am informed that the light has now faded and that this session of the Senate is adjourned. And given the plans for our most august Emperor Decius Messius Quintus Trajanus to confront the enemies of the Empire on our Dacian border, the Senate is excused from its duties for the next month,"

Gaius bowed to the chair and gathered his toga. As he passed Marcus and Demaratus he smiled and quietly remarked, "Aelia's brother chose fools for allies. You will give her my best wishes? Tell her I will stop by and see her tomorrow."

"We will certainly do so, senator, and you have our thanks," said Marcus. The man nodded and passed into the crowd surrounding the Curia.

Demaratus was scanning the crowd, but he could not locate Julius. "He left in a hurry," he observed to Marcus.

"I am not surprised. This was a humiliating experience for him," said Marcus, "But given his wealth and his enmity, he is still dangerous."

“Maybe,” said Demaratus, “But not today, sir, not today.”

“Maybe,” said Demaratus, “But not today, sir, not today.”

XXX

Marcus and Aelia lay in bed, facing one another. Like everyone else in the domus, they had been drained by the events
of the past few days, from the assassination attempt to yesterday's Senate meeting. In the increasingly hot and muggy Roma
climate, they had stripped down to a simple linen supparus slip
for Aelia and a subligarculum loin cloth for Marcus.

"Is it over?" said Aelia softly, tracing Marcus's cheek bones
with an index finger.

"I wish, my love," replied Marcus, "but I fear not."

"Why?" she asked, continuing to trace his face. "Because the
Senate never had an opportunity to vote?"

Marcus sighed. "There is that, yes. Your brother could always
try again, or the emperor could overrule the will. We could even
have a new emperor," he said, "They come and go with some regularity these days." He paused. "And there is something else."

Aelia raised herself on an elbow. "What?"

Marcus rolled onto his back and stared at the ceiling. "The
battle with the Franks was not an invasion. It was ordained."

"What do you mean, 'ordained'"?

"That the Frankish army marched through the heart of Gaul without ever encountering a legion is simply impossible. The legions are no longer massed on the borders as they were in the past. That defense in depth allows them to concentrate quickly in the case of a border incursion. A large number of Franks or Goths or whomever can cross the border, but within a few days they would face a legion, if not several," he said. "The Franks we fought passed right by Norbo, where the VI Legion Victrix is headquartered."

Aelia frowned. "But why would they allow that to happen?"

"I am not sure," he replied. "But I believe the destruction of the VII Legion was its goal."

"The Franks invaded to destroy the VII Legion?" asked Aelia skeptically.

"No, the Franks invaded seeking land in Mauretania, but those who aided them had other goals in mind," opined Marcus.

"But why would someone want to destroy the only legion protecting Hispania?" asked Aelia.

"That 'someone' would like to run Hispania and Gaul, and maybe even Britannia, free from the constraints of the Empire," explained Marcus. "It's someone who aspires to their own empire."

She sat straight up. "Who?"

Marcus shook his head. "I don't know. I am only just beginning to understand your province."

Aelia gave him a lopsided smile. "'Your province?'" she scoffed.

Marcus grinned at her. "Yes, and now mine," he said, reaching for her and pulling her down to him. She snuggled against his neck. "Who is behind all this?" she repeated.

He stroked her hair softly. "That is what I need to find out when we return, but I think it extends to Roma."

She looked up at him, searching for answers she knew could only be partial. "How?"

"Roma knows what it means to march an army the size of the Frankish forces through two provinces without resistance," ventured Marcus. "But if there is an investigation going on, I am not aware of it. I have been here in the capitol for three weeks, and not a single official has shown any interest in discussing it."

"I can see how people in Gaul and Hispania might want to break away from the Empire, but why people here in Roma? That makes no sense. A breakaway would weaken the Empire," she said.

"There are those who make decisions based not on what is good or bad for the Empire, but on how they would personally profit. Can you think of someone like that?" he asked. It wasn't really a question.

"By the gods," she exclaimed, sitting up again.

"A man who would sell his sister into slavery would not think twice about betraying the Empire," said Marcus. "And I cannot believe he is alone. Julius is too calculating to do something of this nature by himself."

Aelia shook her head in agreement. "And too much the coward."

She was silent for a long time. "So, this is not over, is it?" she said.

Marcus shook his head. "No."

"I will help, my love," she said. "You are a newcomer to Hispania, but my family has been there since the end of the

Second Punic War. I will draw on my contacts and we will find out who hides in the shadows and sends barbarians to terrorize and kill our citizens,"

Marcus grinned, "You sound like one of those senators," he teased.

"But what of you, Marcus?" she said, changing the subject. "Who will command the VII Legion?"

Marcus slowly sat up. "I don't know," he said. "That decision has not yet been made."

Aelia nodded. "We will see what we will see," she said. "In the meantime, it is important for us to return, you to Legio, me to Corduba."

Neither of them said anything for a long while. "That will be difficult," Marcus said, breaking the silence. He was not looking forward to their going off in different directions.

She reached across and touched his chest. "I know," she said softly. "Please know that I want no one else but you. We will find a way to be with one another, at least some of the time."

He nodded, unhappily.

"You will have to go by sea, my love," she said. "Legio to Corduba is a week by sea, but many weeks over land."

Marcus blanched. "I cannot, Aelia."

"Marcus, you were fine until you ran out of poppy juice. We will see you are properly supplied this time," she said, rolling off the bed and reaching for a lightweight stola. "Now we have much to do before we depart."

* * *

Demaratus and Coventina sat in a shaded corner of the garden sipping lemon-infused water.

"What now, my Greek?" asked Coventina, putting down her glass.

Demaratus grimaced. "I don't call you, my Celt," he said.

"You do when you are annoyed," she countered.

"That's because when you are annoying you act like a Celt," he replied. "And remember, we invented the word."

She gave him a wry smile. "So, we didn't exist until the Greeks came along and named us?"

Demaratus shook his head. "No, that is not what, oh...," he said, trailing off, then adding, "You are a difficult woman."

"I agree, so why are we together?" she asked.

"Because we are in love?" Demaratus ventured.

"Is that a question or a statement?" she queried.

"A statement," he said softly.

"Good, then we are in agreement and I will go with you to Legio," said Coventina, The afternoon was young, but it was already getting uncomfortably hot. She picked up her glass and took a sip.

"Part of my reluctance to discuss this with you, my love, is that it means leaving Tarraco to live in an isolated and rather primitive place," said Demaratus.

Coventina laughed. "Isolated? From whom? Not from my own people. The Romans took the land from us to build Legio, but we are still there. As for primitive, well 'primitive' is what I grew up in, Demaratus. I am not losing Tarraco, I am going home." She sat back and looked up at the arbor. "I wonder what my family will think of you?" she mused.

"I imagine I would be greeted as a god," said Demaratus, "After all, we invented you."

Coventina shook her head. "I now understand why the Greeks don't rule the world. You annoy everyone."

"I would not dispute that," grinned Demaratus, leaning forward and kissing her.

* * *

Flavius moved slowly around the room while Rachel, looking concerned, observed his movements. "Don't overdo it," she said.

The optio grimaced. "Walking helps loosen the wound," he said, "And I need to be able to move."

"If you cause it to open, it will bleed, and you will be back on your couch," she warned him.

Flavius sighed. "I hate feeling this way, so...helpless."

"I know," she said quietly. Flavius was usually a rock, and here he was straining to walk a few feet. And yet he was not afraid to show her his vulnerability. It was a side of Flavius that Rachel had discovered on this journey and one she was drawn to. Flavius could be endearing in ways that were not at first obvious. "You need to be patient, Flavius. You will heal in time," she assured him.

The optio took another turn around the room, and then sat on the side of his couch, grateful for the respite. Rachel stood to mop his face, which was streaming with sweat from both the strain of walking and the growing heat of the day.

"I need to get better. We are not through with challenges," he insisted.

"Tell me," she said.

Flavius ran his hands through his hair, marshaling his thoughts. "I don't think Aelia's brother is going to give up trying to deprive her of her inheritance. And the situation with the VII Legion is still undecided. And then...." He stopped and gestured vaguely.

"And then there is you and me," she said quietly.

He nodded. "I wasn't sure how to raise that. I know I am going to have to do lots of things."

"What things, Flavius? she asked, puzzled. "What you need to do is get better."

"Well, I mean you said that there were lots of complexities, and I assumed you meant that was because you are Jewish and I am, well, I don't know, just Roman."

Rachel smiled, "I am a citizen of the Empire as well, optio. As for my being Jewish, how is that a problem?"

Flavius looked uncomfortable. "Ah, Demaratus said there were things I needed to do, like find out what you believed in, and then, ah, well, he said there was this covenant, and I needed to have an operation, and then...," he flushed and trailed off.

She laughed. "You think you need to be circumcised?" She shook her head. "Flavius, there are many kinds of Jews. We all believe pretty much the same thing, principally that there is one god, whose name we don't say out loud, and that our religion comes from a book called the Torah. But after that, it gets complex. There are some who live every moment of their life by the words of the Torah. There are some who have barely read it. What binds us together is that our mothers were Jewish and that that we share a history of oppression. I am Jewish, but I don't pay a lot of attention to the Torah. I celebrate our holidays and our traditions, but I do not live my life by a book, and," she added, "you don't have to be circumcised. But if we have children, and they are males, then I will insist on it."

"But you said things were complex?" said Flavius. "Those things are not complex."

"I didn't mean my being Jewish was complex. Well, it is complex, but only for Jews. What I meant was my life is complex. I live in Corduba with Aelia and that makes things complicated," she explained.

"Oh," said Flavius, with obvious relief. "I go where Marcus is, and Marcus and Aelia are together."

"But I don't think Aelia will leave Corduba to live in Legio," said Rachel. "She has talked about Legio, and it is clearly not her choice of abode."

Flavius shook his head. "I think we can sort things out. I don't have all the answers right now, and we can't even think how things will play out without first talking with Marcus and Aelia. But that is just a logistics problem, and those always have a solution. The important thing is that we have an agreement."

Rachel nodded. "I have had no interest in men for a long time, Flavius. But you interest me. I am not entirely sure why, but you are more complex than is apparent at first sight."

"You mean when I was lying on the ground in that Mauri tent with your spear at my throat?" said Flavius with a grin. "But I don't know about complex. With me, you pretty much get what you see."

Rachel laughed. "That scene in the tent was an interesting introduction, but that is not what I mean. Many men never show that they are uncertain or vulnerable. They must always be in charge. You are not like that, Flavius. On the outside you are a disciplined soldier. On the inside, more a human being. That is what I am drawn to."

Flavius put his hands out and Rachel crossed the room to take them. "We will work this out, Rachel." She nodded and sat next to him on the couch, resting her head on his shoulder. He put his arms around her and both sat quietly for a long time.

Life was complex, but also simple.

XXXI

Senator Gaius Julius adjusted his toga and lifted his glass for more wine. A young slave refilled the glass from an ornate gold and silver jug. Next to him sat Emperor Trajanus Decius, who waved the slave away from refreshing his own goblet and leaned forward to watch the chariots rounding a bend in the Circus Maximus. The two were seated on a wide balcony in the Imperial Palace overlooking the huge structure, its benches packed with tens of thousands of spectators. The men could hear the cheers of the crowd, although the palace was hundreds of yards away.

The emperor was slim and bald, with deep lines etched on his brow and cheeks. His mouth was set in a grimace, and he seemed tense and impatient.

"Have you made your preparations, sire?" asked the senator.

Decius sighed. "There is always something that needs to be done, but I plan to leave in the next few days, regardless. The news from the frontier is not good."

"Is it a major invasion, sire?"

"It is hard to say with the Goths. It might be, or maybe just a deep raid. In any case, we need to teach the barbarians a lesson," replied the Decius. "However, I did not call you here to talk about Goths, Gaius."

"Sire?"

"I am concerned about Gaul, senator, and I would like to hear your views. How did a large Frankish army march through one of our provinces without challenge?" queried the emperor, turning from the chariot race and looking at his companion.

"Good question, sire, and most timely. The man who defeated that army is here in Roma and just survived an attempt on his life."

Decius sat up. "Explain," he said.

"Marcus Favonius is the acting legate of the VII Legion Hispania, sire, the army that forced the capitulation of the Frankish army and lifted the siege of Tarraco. He and his companions were set upon yesterday by a gang of assassins following the Festival of Mars," said the senator. "The assassins failed, but they wounded his second-in-command."

"Who is behind this?" asked Decius, "and why is that family name familiar?"

"The Favonius family supported you against Philip, sire. One of the brothers was killed in a confrontation with the Praetorian Guard."

"Ah, yes. Of course. I even spoke with the Guard's legate, Aeilus Hadrianus, about the matter. He claimed the Guard had no choice but to follow Philip's orders to arrest the man, but he was embarrassed about the whole incident, and there were no efforts to arrest any other members of the family. But was the Guard behind this latest attack?"

"No, sire. It appears that Marcus Favonius was not even the target of the assassination. It was his companion, Aelia Dasumi, they were trying to kill."

"Dasumi? The Dasumi family from Hispania? I knew her father when I was governor of the province. A good man. Why was she the target. And again, by whom was she targeted?"

"We are not certain, sire, but it appears her brother was behind the attack. He is disputing the will their father left that evenly divided his wealth between the brother and the sister. The Emperor Gordian approved it and the Senate endorsed it," answered Gaius. "The brother appealed to the Senate, but the senators did not act on it."

"And why was that?" asked the emperor.

Gaius spun his wine glass in his hand and looked up at the ceiling. "It seems that pressing issues about wheat and wool took up the time of the Senate, and the matter was tabled."

Decius chuckled. "Wheat and wool? That wouldn't have been one of your strategies regarding procedural rules at work, would it, senator?

"I think the matter of wheat and wool is profoundly important. I only regret that I did not get to the subject of animals for the games," said Gaius.

The emperor laughed out loud. "You are ever the master of the Senate, sir."

Gaius took a small bow.

"Can we prove the brother ordered this attack?" asked Decius.

"I think not, sire. And to do so would create, ah, difficulties. The man who organized the assassination can be useful on occasion. The whole matter was a debacle. The three women with the party killed two of the assassins and the others fled. The brother is humiliated," said Gaius.

"Women?"

"Yes. It appears the assassins were not prepared to do battle with a bunch of Hispanic Amazons," said Gaius.

"Delicious," said the emperor, "So the attack was not aimed at this legate?"

"No, sire, but it is to our advantage to make it so," said Gaius.

"Explain," directed Decius.

"Word is out that the commander of the VII Legion was attacked, a man who is hailed in Hispania as a hero. And the VII Legion has a history that we much admire. Its full title is the VII Hispanis Gemina Pia. 'Pia' means it is loyal to the Empire."

"What does this have to do with my question about the Franks?" said Decius with a trace of impatience.

"It is my opinion—and I am not alone in this—that the Franks were allowed to march through Gaul without opposition as part of a plot to destroy the VII Legion. Why destroy the VII Legion? Because of that word 'pia,' sire. The VII is the only regular legion in the province, and somebody wanted to get rid of it."

Decius pondered the possibilities. "Who?" he finally pressed.

"We don't know, sire. We are making efforts to find out. But the only reason I can think of is that someone who would like to build their own empire in Gaul, and maybe even in Hispania, saw the VII Legion as an impediment."

"And all this is happening while the Goths threaten our borders in the east," exclaimed Decius. "I can't believe those events are not connected. While we fight the Goths, someone in Gaul dares to seize the opportunity to break away from the Empire."

"That is how I see it, sire, and that is why I supported the Dasumi woman. She is the companion of Marcus Favonius," added the senator.

Decius raised an eyebrow. "My, this does get intricate. It is sounding more and more like good theater."

"Yes, sire, and might I suggest that this Marcus Favonius is our friend in this matter. He is currently acting legate of the VII Legion and waiting to see if he is formally appointed. The current legate is too sick to command."

"Hmmm. And making this Dasumi woman an ally is not a bad move either. Her family is wealthy and influential."

"I should mention that the Vestal Virgins have endorsed the status quo in regards to the Dasumi will," reported Gaius.

"Really?"

"Yes. A generous donation to the Virgins by the Dasumi woman was helpful in that regard," replied the senator.

Decius laughed. "And who suggested that?"

"As you know, sire, I am deeply committed to the Virgins and their tasks," said Gaius solemnly.

Decius sat quietly, watching the climax of the chariot race. As the winner was being festooned with flowers, he turned to the senator. "It seems politic to endorse the action of the Virgins in regards to this will and to appoint Marcus Favonius legate of the VII Legion."

"A wise course of action, sire," agreed the senator.

"One more glass of wine, Gaius, and then begone. I have more to do that you can begin to imagine."

Glossary of Terms

Arivals: Priests who oversaw agricultural fertility

Acta diurnas: Official notices on public boards throughout the city

Century: Basic administrative and military unit of a legion

Cohort: Basic tactical unit of the legion

Centurion: Commander of a century

Domus: House

Gladius: Short stabbing sword of the Roman infantry

Haruspices-Priests who predicted the future based on animal entrails

Legate: Commands a legion

Optio: Second-in-command of a century

Praetorian Guard: Emperor's personal legion, the only legion allowed in Rome

Pugio: Short dagger

Signifer: Officer who carries the century standard, and also oversees the unit's books and the men's pay

Tesserarius: The most junior officer in a century, oversees assigning guard duty

Tribune: Senior staff officer in a legion

Vigiles: Served as police and firemen in cities

Place Names

Roman Names/ Modern names

Aegyptus/ Egypt
Corduba/ Cordoba
Gaul/ Modern France
Legio/ Leon
Mauretania Caesarienis/ Algeria
Aegyptus/ Egypt
Mauretania Tingitana/ Morocco
Narbo/ Narbonne
Tarraco/ Tarragona
Tortosa/ Tortosa

Rivers and Seas

Mare Internum/ Mediterranean
Pontus Euxinos/ Black Sea
Erythra Thalassa (Greek)/ Red Sea
Pontus Herculis (Latin)/ Red Sea
Mare Erythraean/ Indian Ocean
Danuvius/ Danube

Roman Currency

Aureus (gold)
Denarius (silver)
Sestertius (brass)

1 aureus equals 25 denarii
1 denarius equals 100 sestertii

A legionnaire makes 675 denarii a year
A tessarius makes 1012 denarii a year
An optio and a signifer make 1350 denarii a year
A centurian makes 8333 to 15,000 denarii a year
A legate makes 33,333 denarii a year

For comparisons, five denarii buy two gallons of wheat, or 20 loaves of bread. Romans ate two pounds of bread a day. Boots would cost 15 denarii, women's fashionable slippers 20 denarii. A sestertius would buy a pint of middling wine. A pound of purple dyed quality silk can go for 100,000 denarii, the cost of six slaves. A house in a good area of Roma will run 500,000 denarii.

Structure of a Roman Legion

A Roman legion was designed to be a tactically flexible fighting force. To enhance that flexibility, it was divided into discrete units. In that way, a legion resembled a modern infantry division, which is divided into brigades, battalions, regiments, companies and squads. The legion's units could act independently of one another, so that they could reinforce a unit that was in trouble, exploit a weakness in the enemy's line, or block an attempt to outflank the legion. Mobility was the essence of a legion's tactics and made it virtually invincible for almost 700 years. Modern armies owe much of their organizational structure to the Roman legion.

A legion was constructed as follows:

Contubernium: An eight-man squad, the smallest unit in a legion.

Century: Made up of 10 contuberniums. A century is normally 80 men, commanded by a centurion.

Cohort (regular): Composed of six centuries, approximately 480 men.

First Cohort: Composed of five centuries, but each century is composed of 160 men. A First Cohort would be approximately 800 men.

Legion: Made up of 10 cohorts. When headquarters units are included, plus specialists, a legion would be approximately 5,400 men.

Legate: Legion commander.

Tribune: Senior legion staff officer (normally three per legion).

Prefect (Praefectus castrorum): third in command.

Bibliography

The Roman Empire: From Severus to Constantine, by Pat Southern, Routledge, 2001

The Grand Strategy of the Roman Empire: From the First Century AD to the Third, by Edward N. Luttwak, Johns Hopkins University Press, 1979

The Romans in Spain, by John S. Richardson; Blackwell, 1998

War and Society in Imperial Rome: 31 BC-284 AD, by Brian Campbell, Routledge, 2002

Imperial Rome, by Moses Hadas, Time-Life Books, 1965

The Complete Roman Army, by Adrian Goldsworthy, Thames & Hudson, 2003

The Penguin Historical Atlas of Ancient Rome, by Chris Scarre, Penguin, 1995

Handbook to Life in Ancient Rome, by Lesley Adkins and Roy A. Adkins, Oxford University Press,1994

A History of Rome, by Marcel Le Glay, Jean-Louis Voisin &
Yann Le Bohec, Blackwell, 2001

Wars of the Romans in Iberia, by Appian (translated by J.S.
Richardson), Aris & Phillips LTD, 2000

Ancient Rome On Five Denarii A Day, by Paul Matyszak,
Thames & Hudson, 2008

The Making of the Roman Army: From Republic to Empire, by
Lawrence Keppie, University of Oklahoma Press, 1984

The Mammoth Book of Eyewitness Ancient Rome, ed. Jon E.
Lewis, Carrol & Graff Publishers, 2003

Ships and Seafaring in Ancient Times, by Lionel Casson, University of Texas Press, 1994

Roman Social Relations, by Ramsay MacMullen, Yale University Press. 1974

Children of the Empire, by Dalu Jones, Minerva, March/April
2022

In Search of an Antidote for Poisonous Mushrooms, by Alia Katsnelson, *New York Times*, May 16, 2023

Poisons, Poisoning, and the Drug Trade in Ancient Rome, by Dr.
Louise Cilliers, Brewminate, July 30, 2021

Scalpel, Forceps, Bone Drill: Modern Medicine in Ancient Rome, by Franz Litz, *New York Times*, June 13, 2023

"Garum Masala," by William Dalrymple, *New York Review of Books*, April 20, 2023

Ancient Rome: Past and Present Vision, by R.A. Staccioli, 1990.

Acknowledgements

This book could not have been written without the careful copy editing of Anne Hallinan, Betsy Wootten, John Isbister and Roz Spafford, as well as their critiques and suggestions. Danny Hallinan was the book's historical editor, and Jack Radey gave valuable advice on the Roman Army and ancient warfare. My thanks to Ann Higgins for the cover design and to Caroline Jennings for interior formatting and final editing.

Conn M. Hallinan was a long-time columnist for Foreign Policy in Focus, and an independent journalist. For 23 years he oversaw the journalism program at the University of California at Santa Cruz, where he won the UCSC Alumni Association's Distinguished Teaching Award, the UCSC Innovations in Teaching Award, and the Excellence in Teaching Award. He holds a PhD in Anthropology from the University of California, Berkeley and currently resides in Berkeley, CA. Roma, Book IV in the Middle Empire Series, is his fourth fictional work.